BLACKWOOD ESTATES

WILLIAM HOLLOWAY

JOURNALSTONE
YOUR LINK TO ARTIST TALENT

ISBN: 978-1-950305-48-3 (sc)
ISBN: 978-1-950305-49-0 (ebook)
Library of Congress Control Number: 2020938045

First printing edition: September 4, 2020
Published by JournalStone Publishing in the United States of America.
Cover Design and Layout: Don Noble / Rooster Republic Press
Editing by Sean Leonard
Proofreading and Interior Layout by Scarlett R. Algee

JournalStone Publishing
3205 Sassafras Trail
Carbondale, Illinois 62901

JournalStone books may be ordered through booksellers or by contacting:
JournalStone | www.journalstone.com

I'd like to dedicate this story to Michael Louis Lierzer. I miss you. Rest easy, brother.

In the Space Between the Spaces, you will find
All the things God left behind.
All the masks to be torn aside
Do not obscure, they do not hide
All things laid bare: the why, the where
The fire, the smoke, the child's nightmare
And you may ask, and the truth may tell:
This place is not heaven, this place is not hell
But where are we? What is it we see?
No time, no space, no you, no me.

—Louis Villefort, *L'espace entre les espaces*
   (trans. William Holloway)

BLACKWOOD
ESTATES

CHAPTER ONE

PHIL NADA WALKED THE DOG while the nurse tended to his son. He needed these brief interludes to stay sane, because the life he lived wasn't one that he'd prepared for. His life was, by turns, far greater and worse than he'd ever anticipated.

Phil was a best-selling author.

He wasn't John Grisham or James Patterson, but he was a "Big Six" guy, something that he'd never considered a possibility—mainly because he'd never even thought of trying until that fateful day when he'd run into his old buddy Jason Salvato at the grocery store. Jason had gotten signed to a Big Six New York publisher the year before and they paid him $300,000 for his book.

Phil asked Jason how he did it and Jason told him the God's honest truth: Write what most people really want to read. As brain dead as it sounded, Phil hadn't ever considered that before. He was a C-list horror writer, at best. He had written five novels, two self-published and three with specialty horror publishers. He worked tech support on the night shift and wrote when he wasn't helping someone in Australia fix their computer. He went to horror conventions and set up a booth. Reviewers said he was gritty and original, tense and provocative. But he'd never thought that he'd sell enough books to quit his day (or night) job.

While he and Jason browsed the cereal aisle, Jason laid it out for him. People don't read genre fiction, at least not enough of them to justify thinking that one could ever make a living at it—and certainly not a good enough living to raise his son.

On the way home from that conversation at the grocery store, Phil thought hard about the long haul. He was comfortably lower-middle-class. He made enough to pay the mortgage on his little house on the East Side; his wife, Casey, worked at a bookstore. Together they squeaked by, but his two-year-old son would end up going to some pretty tough schools in a few years.

In a flash of inspiration, Phil realized that *he* could write a book that people would be interested in. He shouldn't write about zombies or aliens or mutants or cannibals or other things most people don't want to read about. So he drove to the bookstore, ostensibly to surprise his wife at lunch, but really to have a good hard look at the books on those shelves.

The store she worked at didn't even have a section specifically for horror. The science fiction and fantasy section was decent-sized, but he didn't write the kinds of books that ended up on the shelves at Barnes and Noble. However, the romance, mystery, and thriller sections were pretty darn huge. And that's what Jason had written.

A *thriller*. Complete with international intrigue, bank robbers, computer hackers, and a damsel in distress. A hot damsel who happened to wear leather pants and sought to avenge the death of her father.

While Phil looked down on that sort of thing, he had to admit that those story ideas were easier to come by than C-list horror and sci-fi. Probably because the real world was a dangerous place, full of violence and even more violence.

He walked over to the magazine section, and a headline on the front of *Texas Monthly* caught his eye. It said in big bold letters: "RIP CREWS! TERROR IN NOGALES." It was an article about guys who rob drug mule convoys on the U.S. border with Mexico.

In just the hour since his conversation with his old writer pal, Phil Nada already had a story premise for a thriller. Later that night he watched a special report about a vigilante ex-Army Ranger, a veteran of both Iraq and Afghanistan. He was going to prison for laying waste to the gangbangers plaguing his neighborhood.

And now Phil had his hero.

Six months later he handed his novel, called (unsurprisingly) *Rip Crew*, to Jason, who handed it to his agent. The agent handed it to the publisher, and they handed Phil a check for a half-million dollars.

And that's when his life went sideways.

That was about two and a half years ago. Now he walked Benny, his German Shepherd, and tried to fit all the pieces together in his mind. On the surface, he was all good, but beneath it was another story.

He'd never had any money before, at least not any *real* money, and hadn't appreciated how it could both elevate and disintegrate a man.

The second that he'd gotten the check, both he and his wife had quit their jobs, and within days they were signing the papers on new cars and a McMansion in North Austin. They left their furniture, dishes, everything in their old house on the East Side. Their son Scotty was going to go to a very nice school with the children of software engineers and dentists.

10

They'd spent more than half of his advance before he'd ever sold a single book.

But something about money in hand had done terrible things to Casey.

Gone was the sweet and mousy bookworm in cardigans and Birkenstocks. She'd been replaced by her own opposite, the exact sort of person that terrorized mousy girls who worked at bookstores. An uptight, expensively-clad bitch in a BMW who wanted you to know that she had arrived, and that you'd better ask how high when she said jump.

But it wasn't really even this that sealed the deal for Phil. It was that she started having "girl's nights out" with other high-maintenance women in BMWs, at expensive, glitzy, crass bars downtown, drinking till hey closed, and then driving home.

Lacquered nails and a lacquered mind.

When are you finishing your next damn book?

Have you talked to your agent?

What does the publisher say?

Why don't you want me to be happy and have friends?

I deserve this!

And that's when Scotty was diagnosed with autism. Scotty would not, in fact, be going to that nice school with the children of software engineers and dentists.

Phil asked Casey to refocus her life on Scotty, and Casey said Phil was suffocating her with all of his unreasonable demands, and filed for divorce. She got custody of Scotty, but he lived with Phil at the big empty house in Blackwood Estates. She showed up about once a week to "visit" her son. After he'd learned that these visits would be no longer than an hour, Phil just took Benny out for a walk. He knew that when he walked back through the door, Tawana, their in-home nurse, would be in tears.

The only good thing that Phil got out of the whole deal was his dog. Good old Benny and their walks. His time to pull it together, time to stay sane.

CHAPTER TWO

PHIL HAD LIVED IN TEXAS his whole life, so one hundred degrees was nothing to him.

He found it disappointing that he didn't see more kids out. When he was young and summer was in bloom he'd stayed out all day biking, skateboarding, and raising hell. Kids these days didn't seem to do that, at least not most of them. They seemed, well, really wimpy. It was easy to understand why. They sat in front of computers all day in the air conditioning and drank sodas.

He'd drunk a gallon of soda a day when he was a kidm and lived on Snickers bars and McDonalds. He'd been razor-thin until his mid-twenties. Kids these days didn't exercise. They barely even went outside. Fat was the new normal.

So when he and Benny were on their mid-morning walk, Blackwood Estates was a ghost town of blocky houses on unnaturally green lawns, the only sound being the *kiss-kiss-kiss* of automated sprinkler systems. Sometimes he saw a housewife in an SUV pulling in or out of a driveway, but that was about it.

Except for Lloyd H. Reynolds, Esquire.

That gross old weirdo hung out in his front yard all day watering his maniac flower garden and grinning like a freak. But the way out to the trails behind Blackwood Estates went past his house, so there was no avoiding him. And Benny liked to sniff Lloyd's foliage. Given Lloyd's oozing and unctuous joy at this, Phil wondered if Lloyd would have Benny sniffing more than just flowers if Phil wasn't around.

He was always wearing a purple bathrobe while watering his flowers, which he seemed to do all day.

And grinning.

Lately, as the long-haul fact of his divorce began setting in, Phil had begun the internal discussion of getting out and meeting women. He'd even tried talking to a few online, but author groupies were completely psycho. When he'd been a C-list horror novelist he'd had a regular following of mental patient-grade women emailing him. They were just so nuts and he'd been so in love with Casey that he'd never given it a second thought.

Now, when one of the many SUV-driving housewives drove by he'd smile and wave. He'd seen most of them. Most were pretty well put together. He was even pretty sure some of them were single. He was also sure he looked like a beta male whose best friend was a dog. And they always seemed to drive by while he was making painfully uncomfortable small talk with Lloyd while Benny sniffed the begonias.

So, while Lloyd was fruitily gibbering something to Benny while he nosed through the greenery, Phil tried to look nonchalant as White Escalade Blonde From Over by the Trails drove by. He waved. He always waved. That one always drove by to observe him and Benny and Lloyd with a skeptical glance. Her or Prius Latina in Reflector Shades Listening to Metallica.

Neither of them ever waved back, but they drove past none the same while Lloyd groped Benny.

"Don't worry, Phil, it'll be our little secret." Lloyd showed too much gum while grinning. *If you don't stop that you might sprain your face, you fucking freak.*

"What do you mean, Lloyd?"

"You and Mrs. Simmons. Blondie in the yoga pants."

"Blondie in the yoga pants?"

Phil knew what he was talking about and was doing a poor job with nonchalance. Despite that fact that it was Lloyd saying it, White Escalade Blonde From Over by the Trails in yoga pants was enough to make him run home for a cold shower.

"Yeah, Mrs. Simmons. And yes, she's single. Her husband is a programmer over in Westlake."

"Uh, okay, good seeing you, Lloyd."

"The divorce isn't finalized. It was amicable, he's just a big ol' flaming queen and needed to be free!"

He said this with a ridiculous little hopping flourish and a flapping of his icky chicken arms right in time for Prius Latina in Reflector Shades Listening to Metallica to drive by from the other direction. Her expression went from amusement to hilarity.

Phil went to a bright reddish purple color.

"Oh, and that's Esme Salazar. Her and her fat bigot husband have *Republican* signs up in their yard 24/7. I don't get it. Do they think the

13

Republicans want tacos that bad? It makes me madder than Republican blacks thinking they can be the house n—"

"Lloyd. I really gotta go."

"Oh. Okay then, see you."

But Phil was already halfway down the block, angling toward the corner where he'd turn down Maypole Street, which dead-ended into the trails. He'd had enough of Lloyd for the day. Knowing that the old perv was a *racist* old perv was just too much. He'd called someone a bigot, then felt completely comfortable splashing out the lingo. What a guy.

And now Phil would be walking past Escalade Blonde's house. *Mrs. Simmons.*

Hers was the last house on the right, then the forest and the trails. There was a little knee-high traffic barrier. All you had to do was step over it and you were on the trail. It took a left past her driveway where her big white Escalade sat most of the time.

The trails went all the way out to Parmer Lane and branched off throughout the woods. At Parmer, it went up behind the big roller rink. Phil was really looking forward to taking Scotty there, as silly as it sounded, but that was before they found out about the autism, before they found out about the seriousness of the autism.

Before *he* found out. He was pretty convinced that Casey no longer gave a flying fuck about Scotty. Money did weird things.

But enough of that. He was here to clear his head, not dig himself a deeper hole in there. He already did that enough, writing about the things he did, all the while with Scotty and Benny and Tawana playing around him. The things he wrote about were rough: Islamic terrorism, WMDs going off in cities. Writing and researching about that took a bigger chunk out of him than horror ever did.

He smiled just thinking about Tawana. She was a godsend even if she was covered in gang tattoos. She even had a big teardrop inked under her eye, which generally meant that she did some time, but despite that she was perfect with Scotty. They laughed and played all day, and when he had an episode she brought him back from hysteria. She was a skinny little thing, so it was hard to imagine her getting up to enough trouble to get put away for it.

Then another dark thought hit Phil. One day Scotty was going to get a lot bigger. One day Tawana wouldn't be able to control him when he had an episode. One day the inevitable would come and it would be an institution. He stopped in his tracks and fought back the tears.

He didn't want to fight this alone.

Why did you leave me, Casey?

Why did you cut and run?

He wiped his wrist across his eyes and looked down at Benny's big understanding eyes. He didn't give him a fake smile; Benny was a German Shepherd and smart enough to know when Phil was upset. Smart enough to know in what way Phil was upset.

Can a dog give you a reassuring look? A little cock of the head and a shift of the ears?

Phil laughed at himself and reached down to ruffle Benny's fur. "The only good thing that money's ever done for me, ain't that right, boy?"

He bent down and Benny licked the tears from his face.

Phil laughed and looked up.

He'd been doing this little breakdown on the trail right next to Mrs. Simmons's driveway.

A beta male whose best friend was a dog…

Luckily, she wasn't unloading groceries or whatnot, watching the all-American implosion.

She was screaming. Loud, from inside her house. Screaming at a kid. Damn. That kid must be a serious little shit. Or Mrs. Simmons is a world class abuser. One or the other.

Suddenly he wasn't thinking about Scotty or Casey or Benny or himself.

Do I do something?

Sorry, I was just walking past and I heard you abusing your kid, you wanna go out for drinks?

Then Benny got in on the act. His head cocked one way, then the other, and he let out a whining yelp. This was his *Now I'm totally confused* bark. It also had an edge of fear to it. Benny was a big dog, with both obedience and attack training. The reason that the cops used German Shepherds is that they wre trainable and smart, both intuitive and curious. He could read people like an open book.

Benny wasn't stupid, and he was basically fearless.

Why was there a hint of fear in that weird little yelp?

Why is he now running a circle around me, tangling me in the leash?

That, specifically, is something Benny doesn't do.

"Hey, boy, what's that all about? What's gotten into you?"

Just as easily as he'd tangled Phil's legs in the leash, he untangled himself and headed back the way they came from. Back toward the house, not out to the trails. He turned and looked back and gave a single bark.

I'm letting you know that it's important to follow me now.

"What? It's walk time, Benny. And God knows we need some free time. At least, I need some time…"

Benny gave another, more insistent bark and pulled on the leash.
Seriously, we need to go home.

"Benny, c'mon. There ain't a bear out there. Just grass and trees and a roller rink, and whatever her"—motioning toward Mrs. Simmons's house—"deal is…it'll sort itself out."

Benny gave him a reproachful look and assented. Training overrode whatever his instincts told him.

Phil stepped over the little traffic barrier with a single look over his shoulder at Mrs. Simmons's house. The screaming had stopped, but it still worried him. Either she or her kid were seriously in need of something.

As soon as they hit the trail, Benny's odd behavior kicked up a gear. Ordinarily it was all tail wagging and sniffing every square inch of everything that could be sniffed.

Phil reached down and detached the leash from his collar. That was one of the beautiful things about Benny's training. He didn't run far enough to let his master out of his sight. He chased rabbits, but Phil never had to chase Benny. When he bought Benny, he did so with an ulterior motive. He knew he was a fuck up, but that Benny wouldn't be. Benny would be better than the man who owned him. He could own something better than himself.

Benny didn't move from Phil's side. His ears were pointed up and his head roved from side to side, checking all the angles.

Phil sighed and led the way. It was humid, maybe something was in the air, something that smelled off to Benny, maybe it was the…
Clouds.

Okay, yeah, that qualifies as weird. When Phil walked out the front door the sky was pure blue; now it was a flat slate of grey-white cloud. And something about the way the horizon *folded in* was strange too. It looked like the horizon ended about a mile or less away, not the usual fifty.

But the weather can turn on a dime in Texas. The humidity may have hit some sort of critical mass and formed clouds. Phil searched his brain, then had to stop. He didn't actually know how that sort of thing worked. He just knew the clouds were here, the horizon looked weird, and Benny didn't care for it one bit.

"Okay, boy, I think I get it. You think we're about to have some kinda weather."

He reached down and stroked Benny's neck and ears.

"Maybe we'll have a tornado, is that it, boy?"

There was zero wind. Wasn't that supposed to happen right before a tornado?

Phil didn't know the answer to this one either, just that he needed to get a move on if he was going to get his requisite distance in for the day. Years ago he'd decided that he didn't want to look like the other guys. C-list horror writers tended to be fat, bald, bespectacled, and share an affinity for halitosis. Phil exercised, brushed his teeth, and didn't wear glasses, even though he was getting more convinced that his vision wasn't what it used to be.

Besides, Phil wasn't one of those guys anymore.

He was respectable, legit, right?

Phil sighed and shook his head again. Those clouds were convincing him that it was indeed time to go get his vision checked.

They continued their walk down the trails toward Parmer, going into the thicker trees toward the rear of the roller rink. With every step Benny's state of alert increased and Phil's unease rose with it.

Everything felt wrong. There was buzzing just this side of the audible range and the air went dry, not humid. It was sudden too, a whispering whoosh, and the little hairs on his arm stood up. It was supposed to be humid, that's just the way the weather was here. Now it was dry.

Dry and buzzing.

Even breathing felt awkward. It dried his mouth instantly and his lips felt chapped, but it was the middle of summer. The only thing that seemed normal was the temperature. It was hot, really hot, probably 110 degrees.

By the time the trail branched off to the rear of the roller rink he had decided to turn around and go home. He and everyone complained about the humidity, but he never imagined how it would feel for the humidity to drop to zero. And what the hell was that damn electrical buzzing? It seemed to come from all directions, but always remained the same distance away from him.

He stepped up the little incline to the service alley behind the Roller Palace.

He was parched. He decided in this moment that he'd never truly been parched before, that the word itself sounded exactly how his breath sounded going in and out of his dry mouth.

Parch parch parch parch…

He looked down to Benny to see if he was going through the same thing.

"Benny, we're gonna go around front and hopefully they'll give us a Coke on spec. I know you don't like Coke, but…"

Benny was staring into the open loading dock. Nothing interesting back there, just stacks of boxes labeled *Popcorn* and *Cotton Candy Base*,

Cooking Oil and *Bleach*. But Benny was crouched, eyes wide, lips quivering. His tail was pointed up and back, rocking side to side like a metronome in slow motion.

Phil had never seen Benny like this. The closest approximation was during his attack training, where his fury went from zero to sixty in the blink of an eye, and then he was calm and in control the next second. Benny was always calm; other dogs barely registered to him. He was the alpha, and he knew it.

"Whoa, boy, let's just skip that Coke…"

Then Phil noticed the sounds, or rather the sounds that were missing. Parmer was a busy road with a speed limit of 55 miles per hour.

There was no sound of cars.

There was also no sound of birds. There should have been a million grackles back here to scavenge the dumpsters, but there was nothing. *There had also been no regular sounds out on the trails.* He'd just been so perplexed by the buzzing and the odd, instantaneous weather shift that he hadn't even noticed it.

If they double timed it back home, he could be drinking a Topo Chico at his desk in ten minutes. They'd been thirsty on the way, but so far this walk had turned into a sandwich of weird and he didn't like the taste at all. People might claim to like weirdness, but in reality, they don't like it one bit. Phil was no exception.

"Benny, we're gonna go now, so…"

The music thumping through the cinderblock walls stopped. One second, "Don't Stop Believin'" by Journey; the next, nothing.

Then the screaming started. And in seconds it changed, too. Kids, children, screaming without rhyme or reason, a *Walpurgis* riot, then the sound of women shrieking in terror, confusion and agony.

Benny actually hopped back a foot and looked up.

Okay, I warned you, things are bad. Can we go?

Phil looked down, his expression a maze of confusion and fear.

Did a bomb go off in there?

What do I do?

I don't know what makes people sound like that!

Benny made the decision for him. He got behind him, got a mouthful of shirttail, and started pulling Phil back the other direction.

Phil didn't need any more convincing.

"I'll call the cops when I get home!"

And they ran.

18

CHAPTER THREE

PHIL MIGHT HAVE PRIDED HIMSELF on not looking like a fat, bald, bespectacled C-list horror writer with halitosis, but he was really only able to put about two solid minutes of running together. Then he had to stop. Phil was in fair shape, all things considered, but this air was just wrong. It dried out his nose and his eyes and his throat. It tasted dirty and dusty even though there was no wind to stir it up.

The buzzing must be static electricity, he thought. The air was bone dry, and that made for static electricity. It actually seemed to lift dust into the air.

He tried to catch his breath and breathe through his nose.

He pulled out his phone and called Tawana. As soon as he tried, he got the dreaded *no signal* tone. No bars on the signal strength indicator, either. This was getting weirder and weirder. One of the few things he really loved about Blackwood Estates was that he always got a good cell signal. The big relay towers were only a few miles from here and he could see them...if it weren't for the weird canopy of clouds. He hadn't thought about that earlier. If there were overcast skies from horizon to horizon, he'd still be able to see the cell towers.

But he couldn't.

Which must mean that the cloud cover somehow extended to the ground about a mile away at all points of the compass. Like a bowl of clouds had been placed over his part of the world.

Very strange weather and weird screaming.

He tried to laugh it off, but his nose was burning.

"It's all right, boy, ol' Phil's just losing his marbles. Ain't that right, Benny?"

Benny let out an anxious little growl and looked back in the direction of the skating rink.

They heard the mindless screams of one little kid, then another and another. It wasn't a scream of pain. Or an overexcited playground scream. It was screaming for screaming's sake.

Phil had spent a night in jail before. He got a DWI in his early twenties. Got booked around nine and made it into the cells by eleven. Drunks, junkies and crazies. As the hours passed, they got more agitated and wound up. At around three in the morning they started screaming. It was like the monkey house at the zoo. Withdrawal does crazy things.

This sounded like that, but these were little kids.

And it sounded like they were heading this way.

Benny and Phil ran again.

They made it to the trailhead, and Phil held his hand over his nose and mouth as he swung a leg over the little traffic barrier. His nose was still burning from the funky dry air. His eyes, too.

Escalade Blonde was in her driveway, behind the wheel of her Escalade, while a little girl outside the driver's side door slapped at the window. It looked like the little girl had chased Mrs. Simmons there. A full-grown woman, barricaded in an SUV, trapped by a girl no older than six or seven. There were handprints on the pristine white of the driver's side door and window. Bloody prints from bloody little hands.

Both Mrs. Simmons and the little girl turned to Phil and Benny. The little girl's expression wasn't one that Phil had seen before. It was hate and calculation and surprise all at once. It struck Phil that this berserk little girl wasn't even passingly concerned with him; it was Benny that she focused on.

Mrs. Simmons's face registered nothing but loss and uncomprehending fear.

Benny let out a lethal sounding growl and the little girl sprinted away. A second later, Phil heard the sound of a slamming door, then an unhinged ululation from inside the Simmons's house. He had seen some crazy little kids before, but this little girl was a whole other kind of fucked up.

The sounds of screaming were approaching. He could imagine a hundred clones of that crazy little girl pouring out of the loading dock behind the Roller Palace, fanning out through the trails and converging on this spot.

Jesus!

This weather was fucked up and was fucking with his head.

Stress. Divorce. Financial insecurity. A disabled son. *Those* are the things you need to worry about, not weird weather or the Escalade Blonde and her behavioral problem kid, or whatever the hell is going on at the Roller Palace (and spilling out of the Roller Palace and down the trails toward Blackwood Estates on a tide of lunatic children's screaming…).

He looked down to Benny, who kept looking back to the trails and what was approaching in the distance, then back to Mrs. Simmons, who, in turn, was staring at them.

Phil gave a confused half-wave, a sign that he meant no harm, then started walking over. She slammed the Escalade into gear, tires spinning, and raced out of her driveway in reverse. She screeched to a halt, then floored it down Maypole Street, running the stop sign and tearing down Phil's street.

Phil looked down to Benny again.

Benny looked back to the trails and nudged Phil's hand holding the leash.

Okay, put the leash on because we really need to get home now, like right *now.*

Phil nodded, confusion and fear stamped on his face. He clipped on Benny's collar and they began their brisk walk down Maypole.

On the corner of Maypole and Bailey, they met the Smith twins, Denny and Penny. He'd learned their names on one of the occasions he'd been forced into conversation with Lloyd. He didn't know their parents, only that Dad drove a black Suburban and Mom drove a white Suburban.

They were about eight or nine years old and looked exactly alike. Brown hair, bowl cuts, freckles, bright blue eyes. Ordinarily the only way you could tell them apart was the school uniforms, her in a plaid skirt and him in khaki pants and a tie. But there were no uniforms today, just shorts and t-shirts. Phil guessed the one in the pink shirt was Penny and the one in the grey Transformers logo shirt was Denny.

Benny liked them just about as much as he liked everything else so far.

His teeth were bared, his stance a coiled crouch. Despite everything that had been drilled into his head, he was ready to kill these two kids. Phil doubled the leash around his fist.

"Benny, stop that! What has gotten into you today?"

He looked at the kids. "Sorry, kids, ordinarily he's real sweet but it's been a rough day. Just gonna get him home."

Benny obeyed, but stayed at red alert. Then Penny spoke: "He has the wolf under control, does he not?"

Denny answered her: "He does, but this threat is not idle. Much has gone wrong. I do not recognize this place, these engines and fortifications."

Their words stopped Phil in his tracks. He doubled the leash around his hand again and turned back to them. Benny was positively vibrating with fury.

"Benny, heel! Now, sit."

Phil glanced down at him, then back to the kids.

"Kids, are your parents home? Can you run inside and get them for me?"

The twins looked at each other and smiled. They had the faces of children but expressions unlike those of children. Phil was reminded of the grinning of terrorists as they leered at a world shocked by their deeds.

He took a step back and cleared his throat.

"Kids?"

They didn't say anything, but Penny pulled a cellphone from her pocket and looked at it like it was both an object of joy and of utter confusion.

She giggled. "Oh, Mommy! Sweet, sweet Mommy, won't you come and talk to the wolf handler? He's so very interested!"

Phil spoke before thinking: "Kid, you actually gotta dial the phone, it doesn't work that way."

The ghoulish grin fell from Denny's face. Suddenly he was a child again. "It doesn't work here, here isn't here anymore."

Penny's mocking mirth fell away and was replaced by a cold appraisal of Phil and Denny. She put her arm around her brother. "It's okay, we will travel on, and you with us."

Phil was done with this. Done with this weather, done with the weird screaming, done with these evil puppet children. Yep, that's what they looked like: puppets. He didn't have a better approximation.

He glanced down at Benny. "I'm done here, you satisfied?"

Benny looked back to him. *Yeah, and you better start listening, because this isn't over.*

And they walked on down the street. He could see Lloyd, standing out in front of his house, holding his water hose like a big green phallus, spraying down his beautiful flowers. Phil's detestation of Lloyd magnified. He walked to the other side of the street and looked at the ground.

Benny was still at red alert so he didn't tug on the leash to go sniff Lloyd's tulips.

Phil whispered to Benny, "I fucking hate that guy."

But Lloyd wasn't going to be done with them so easily. He was going to call them over and grope Benny and sidle over and…

Even from a few houses down, Phil heard Lloyd's gobbling cry. He looked to see Lloyd covering his mouth with one hand and pointing with the hand holding the hose at something next door, almost directly across the street from Phil's own home.

He couldn't see what he was pointing at, but Lloyd's tone couldn't be faked. Something had really just happened. Phil walked over to his side of the street and stood a few feet from Lloyd to get a better view.

It was the Rosales girls, all three of them, and two other little girls he didn't recognize. The three sisters were in nightgowns, and the other two were in regular little kid summer attire, shorts and t-shirts. The three sisters and one of the other girls each held out a string, and each string was tied to a leg of Edwina, the long-haired calico cat that seemed to be in love with Benny. And Benny seemed to love her back. Phil wasn't sure where she came from, but she was well fed and didn't have fleas, so he didn't really care. The two animals would sit on the back porch and snuggle for hours every day.

But that wasn't going to happen anymore, because the fifth little girl was pulling out Edwina's internal organs. The other four were doing some kind of moaning and groaning, like Tibetan throat singing but coming from the voices of little girls.

Little girls disemboweling a cat.

A living cat, thrashing and screeching.

Blood rained onto the driveway and Edwina went limp.

Phil didn't make a sound, and neither did Lloyd, but an enraged whine turned into a scream of fury from Benny.

The four girls holding the strings connected to the cat's paws dropped them and ran inside their house. The fifth girl, holding the cat's innards, turned to regard them.

Her eyes went from Lloyd to Phil and then to Benny. She spent less than a second on the men, but Benny held her interest.

He fell silent, letting out only an agitated little whimper.

She pointed to him. She spoke some words in a guttural language, then switched to English. "You appear as a servant of Ithaqua, yet you cozen these Sons of Adam. You must be..."

It was Lloyd who silenced her. He rotated the nozzle on his hose and blasted her with a high-pressure stream. Right in the face. She shrieked, this time like a regular little girl, then ran into the house and slammed the door. What about the other four little girls?

Benny made a sound like crying, then sat back on his haunches and let out a long, powerfully sad wailing.

Phil and Lloyd slowly turned to one another.

Phil rapidly nodded his head. "Thanks, Lloyd. That was...that was the right thing to do... I think."

Then his blood ran cold; something was wrong at almost every point of the compass. One way or another, everything was off. The clouds, the air, the buzzing, the screaming. Psychotic children.

Some kind of natural disaster…

Chemical spill…

Chemical *attack*…

Scotty.

Benny was one step ahead, but this time Phil wasn't so far behind. They sprinted the half-block to Phil's house.

He struggled with the keys at the front door. His hands were shaking with fear. How could he have stayed out there so long? Why wasn't his first instinct to rush back to Scotty? What kind of a father was he?

Despite the escalating freak show, in his mind he still said: *A better parent than Casey.*

The air in here was better than outside, but he could tell the AC was off. The ceiling fans weren't spinning, either.

No power.

"Tawana?"

Benny dashed off through the house and started barking up a storm at the back door.

Phil looked to his right into the big living room. This was his office, and this was where Tawana tended to Scotty during the day. Tawana and Benny. Nickelodeon and Cartoon Network. When Scotty took a nap, Tawana switched it to BET.

No one in the living room.

The room was strewn with Scotty's toys. They were toddler toys even though he wasn't a toddler anymore. It was uncertain if he'd progress past that point.

But the usual mess of a child at play wasn't the issue. It was the shattered glass tabletop. It was easy to clean, which was important with a little kid, and tempered so it would be harder than you'd expect to break. It looked like someone fell, or was pushed onto it.

Someone who weighed more than Scotty.

Someone who started bleeding after they got out of the broken glass and staggered into the kitchen, trailing blood over to the back door.

Tawana lay in one of the patio chairs in the back yard.

Benny let out an agonized whine and looked up at the ceiling.

Phil opened the door and walked out to her.

She lay on her side. A long, thin kabob skewer had been shoved through her upper back and poked out the front of her scrubs.

She'd probably been stabbed in the living room, fallen into the table, then somehow gotten up and made it to the back door. She'd had the presence of mind to lock the door behind her, but whoever attacked her didn't pursue her out here.

Phil kneeled down next to her. "Oh fucking Jesus, Tawana…"

She'd gone a pale grey color and blood leaked out of her mouth and drooled to a puddle next to the chair. Phil knew what this color meant. She had cuts and gashes all over her from the broken glass, but only the skewer could account for her color. She was bleeding to death internally.

"Phil, my baby boy, my boy… It ain't him. He didn't do it. Wasn't him, no sir."

Phil touched her hair. A terrible icy fear, worse than anything he'd ever imagined, spread through his limbs. "Tawana, Tawana… Where is Scotty?"

Her eyes shifted from his face to the second story windows behind.

Benny sniffed and licked Tawana's face gently. He knew as well as Phil did that she would be gone in minutes.

An odd, happy smile crossed her face. "White man's dog ain't so bad…"

The frigid fear held Phil's breath hostage.

The unnatural expressions on the kid's faces.

The shrill cry of the cat.

"Tawana, who did this? Was it the little girls from across the street?"

Her strength was fading. "My baby boy. Casey did you wrong, Phil. I'm so sorry. So sorry." And she slipped from consciousness.

She was gone. Phil reached for her wrist to check for a pulse, and it was there, but faint and fading.

Benny let out a long mournful wail and Phil looked at his cellphone. Still no signal, no bars. He looked out to the horizon, much closer than it should have been, and part of him began to suspect that he was in this thing alone. Him and Benny and Scotty, and for the first time in his life, he was going to need to be a better man than he knew how to be.

He looked down to Benny, who didn't look away from the upstairs windows.

"Benny, I don't want to do this."

Benny looked to him. His big brown eyes hadn't lost their steel, but he was devastated, scared, and confused too.

There's no going back.

Phil nodded and they walked in the back door. The air was better in here, though it was becoming unnaturally dry as well.

But it wasn't silent.

"*Cows say mooooooo…*"

Then a winding noise.

"*Pigs say ooooooink…*"

Benny let out an apprehensive little growl. They crossed the glass-strewn living room into the foyer. When they'd run in from their walk, he'd hung Benny's leash out of pure muscle memory.

Now he took the leash and reached over and clamped it on Benny's collar. It just seemed like the right thing to do.

"*Ducks say quack quack quack…*"

Casey had bought that for Scotty from the children's section at the bookstore. They'd read that he should be speaking more than he was at the time, and she'd found this toy. It was called Pharmphonic, and it was supposed to help with teaching speech.

Scotty hadn't outgrown it so far.

"*Horses say naaaayyy…*"

They started up the curving steps and the out of place sounds of Scotty's Pharmphonic accompanied them.

And then they were at his room. It was painted a bright happy green color, with a bright red Spiderman blanket on the bed and Spiderman posters on every wall. Scotty could barely speak, but he loved Spiderman.

"*Cows say mooooooo…*"

Scotty was sitting on the bed, facing the wall, pulling the string on his Pharmphonic.

Phil whispered, "Scotty, are you okay?"

He didn't turn around, he just pulled the string again.

"*Ducks say quack quack quack…*"

Benny barked once. Short, quick, like he did with other dogs to let them know their place.

Scotty turned around, but it wasn't Scotty, at least not entirely. He was hard, cold, and aware in a way that Scotty could never be. He didn't even glance at his father, he just stared at Benny in a kind of furious curiosity. Their gazes remained locked for several moments before Scotty broke away.

Then his eyes closed and his shoulders slumped, his breathing changed, becoming softer and less focused. He opened his eyes again and looked at his father and Benny.

"Bennay, Bennay…"

He gave his dad the optimistic look he always gave him when he wanted to be carried to the bathroom, holding out his arms for his father to pick him up.

Phil breathed a sigh of relief and started toward his son, but Benny pulled back on the leash. He wasn't growling, but his tail was straight and his eyes were wide. He pulled back further, dragging Phil back a step.

Scotty's eyes went back to Benny and his arms dropped to his sides. His shoulders became stiffer, more erect, more formal.

And his eyes...

Phil's breath caught in his throat. Those weren't his son's eyes.

"Scotty, buddy, are you okay?"

He pulled the string on his Pharmphonic and looked at his father, appraising and weighing him.

"Ducks say quack quack quack..."

And then he *spoke*. "This one is not as he should be. How is it that his will is yours?"

Phil's knees gave out, and Benny went to a defensive stance, putting himself in between Phil and Scotty. He still hadn't growled, his training in effect, but he no longer fully saw Scotty as Scotty.

But Phil... He'd never heard his son speak in complete sentences, had come to terms with the damnable truth that he may never hear his son speak more than simple words.

"Oh, Scotty... Oh, dear God, Scotty..."

The child that was, but wasn't, Scotty nodded his head. "His name is Scotty."

Tears poured from the lids of Phil's clenched eyes. "Yes, yes, my boy."

Phil looked up and into the face of his son, but nothing of his son lay behind those eyes. "To hear him speak intelligibly pleases you, because he is a simpleton."

Phil's blood pounded in his ears. He'd never heard a person refer to Scotty in anything other than loving and kind terms; it was much worse to hear the words come from his own son's mouth.

"How could you—"

"Imbecile. Your son is an imbecile, and you..." He smiled with deep satisfaction. "You are a weakling."

CHAPTER FOUR

P HIL'S MOUTH FELL OPEN, AND a wheeze came from his upper chest, like he'd been punched in the sternum. Stars began to streak in the periphery of his vision, and even on his knees he felt too weak. He was going to go to the floor.

Benny sensed this and let out another short bark of warning and establishment of primacy. Benny was still a dog, but he understood king of the mountain better than any human.

Scotty, or the thing in Scotty, recoiled to the corner of the bed, his teeth showing a snarl. As soon as he did, Benny escalated, crouching and poising to spring.

This brought Phil back from his fugue. He pulled the leash. He couldn't budge Benny even if he used all of his strength, but it was a signal. Attacking Scotty, even if something alien was speaking from inside him, was the same as attacking Scotty.

Scotty laughed. Not a happy child's laugh, but the laugh of something wise and old and dead to mercy. "It is a mystery how you aligned with this wolf, but I assure you, it can only injure the halfwit, not me."

Phil stood, his hands shaking, then turned to the door behind him and locked it. He pulled the belt from around his waist. "Benny, we're gonna need to tie up Scotty until EMS gets here."

The Scotty-thing leapt off the bed in an attempt to escape. It was strong, impossibly strong for a child, but clumsy, as if it was somehow unfamiliar with the length of its own limbs. Benny intercepted him with ease, using his vise-like jaws and powerful paws without leaving a scratch on Scotty. He'd been roughhousing with the boy since they could walk, but neither Benny nor Phil had ever heard him screech like this.

He was homicidally enraged, furious at a level impossible for nearly any human save for dedicated sociopaths. He snatched out at throats and eyes. Benny was untouched, but by the time they had Scotty face-down on the carpet with his hands behind him, Phil's arms and face were heavily scratched.

Phil sat back and breathed into his hands. He'd just hogtied his son with a belt and pillowcase around his ankles. Phil thought he felt an anxiety attack coming on—he'd never had one before, but he'd also never had to tie up his son because he might have committed murder before, either.

His breathing became strained. He couldn't get enough air—and the air itself was getting worse. If it was this painfully dry inside the house, it must be really bad outside the house. Benny walked over and licked Phil's face and put his head on his shoulder, then went back to the supine form of Scotty and sniffed his face intently.

Phil wiped the tears from his face and leaned back against the wall. He looked down at his son and found a hard-wizened grimace looking back.

The Scotty-thing smiled grimly. *"Lorsque les étoiles s'alignent, nous ouvrirons une porte sur l'espace entre les espaces."*

Phil ignored this outburst. So many impossible things had happened in the last hour that he couldn't keep track. His autistic son, who had previously had the speech capacity of a two-year-old, had spontaneously adapted the syntax of an educated sociopath from the 1890s, and now French.

Phil didn't know much about languages, but he could pick out French.

He pulled out his cell. Still no bars and a beeping telling him that there was no service. He didn't have a landline. And the electricity was out, so no computer. That left his laptop and his iPad, but if there was no electricity there would be no router, and if there was no cell, there would be no wide area connectivity.

He turned the cell off to conserve the battery. "Scotty, are you okay?"

Something in Scotty's hard expression softened. He rolled over onto his back and lifted his feet in the air, looking at the pillowcase tied around his ankles. He laughed, sounding a little unsure, but it looked like a game to him.

Scotty is in there, but so is some other personality.

As a fiction writer, Phil had read far more information than he actually understood about schizophrenia. Is it possible for someone to spontaneously develop a second personality that happens to talk like Sweeney Todd with a dash of French?

He had to admit, it sounded a whole lot more like *Ancient Aliens* and Zecharia Sitchin stuff, but he didn't want to think about it that way.

29

Maybe the *Book of Enoch* and something about the Watchers?

That's what he really felt, but he wasn't a C-list horror guy anymore. He was a thriller writer. Legit. Respectable and upstanding. Gritty and—

"Dadday?"

Scotty was smiling at him and looking at the belt pinning his arms to his sides.

Benny's ears perked up, and he looked from Scotty to the bedroom door. Phil had come to know Benny's facial expressions and body language pretty well.

Somebody was at the front door.

A cautious growl came from Benny, and Scotty's softness went rigid again. A covert and sly look came over him. The dog looked to the boy and gave a knowing bark.

You're not fooling me.

Scotty, or the personality inside Scotty, gave up on this deception. His expression went to one of intense concentration. He was listening hard for something.

He didn't have to listen for long.

A long, piping ululation of children came from all around the house. It was strained and freakish, a noise that wasn't supposed to come from human vocal chords, like a parrot imitating the human voice.

Benny's hair stood up and he fixed Scotty with dark glare of warning.

Scotty looked back and forth in excitement and shrieked.

Long, loud, and high, another sound that must've hurt to make because it didn't sound as if his throat was made for it. It was more like a whale or an exotic bird. A single sustained note, high and loud and flanged. It was call and response; the pack had called, and he had answered.

So unnatural, so outside of what Phil could be expected to understand, he leapt up and threw his hands over his son's mouth. He should have taken notice of the glee that filled his son's eyes at his approach and the quick tugging in the opposite direction of the leash in his hand.

Scotty's teeth sank into the meat of his middle finger and locked together and his head shook back and forth, tearing flesh from bone.

Phil screamed in agony.

Benny howled in rage.

Scotty screamed in bloody-mouthed joy, sticking his tongue out and displaying the bloody morsel on the tip of his tongue before swallowing it and laughing. It wasn't the laugh of an autistic boy, but that of a man to whom killing was business.

But Phil's screaming and Scotty's laughing couldn't cover Benny's warning barking. *Danger, something is here, right now!*

Downstairs, glass shattered and the mindless screaming that they heard from outside the roller rink began again, now much closer and much louder.

Scotty screamed again, this time the same scream as before—the high-pitched keening— and Phil did something he'd never done before. He slapped Scotty, leaving a bloody splat across his face from the section of his middle finger that had been denuded of flesh.

Scotty was bowled over sideways from the force of the blow, and went down on the carpet, unable to move because of his bonds. For a brief moment his face was vacant, and then Scotty, Phil's son Scotty, came back and began to wail, a lament of confusion and pain.

His boy, his son, was in pain and distress, and Phil wanted nothing more than to hold him and calm him and comfort him, but the shrieking of the intruders was accompanied by the drumroll of many little feet pounding up the stairs, hell-bent on answering the call of the thing inside Scotty.

Phil was still on his knees, mentally reeling, but Benny wasn't. He launched in the opposite direction at the open bedroom door, announcing his presence to the intruders still advancing up the stairs. Phil let go of the leash, and that one action probably saved their lives.

Benny bounded down the hall and down the stairs, causing an avalanche of terrible child attackers. There were five of them, apparently; the ones closest to the house answered the call first. It was the Smith twins, Denny and Penny, and the Rosales girls. The other two little girls— the two that had been with the Rosales girls—were absent.

Down the stairs they went, a tangle of little kids and a tornado of fur named Benny. Their high-pitched shrilling changed to shouts, then to screams of fury, then of pain. There was a furious growling and the receding screams of the children as they ran away, all except for one of them.

Benny trotted back into Scotty's bedroom with a terrified look in his eyes and his face covered in blood.

Phil, I've done something very bad.

CHAPTER FIVE

THE STAIRCASE WAS A RIDICULOUS and ostentatious curving thing visible from the big windows at the sides of the front door. The foyer was grand indeed, with a big glass and brass chandelier, the staircase arcing from right to left with wood-carved handrail posts.

Benny had met the children's charge about three-quarters of the way up, causing a domino effect. Then he got hold of Mary Rosales. She was probably about five years old.

All of his life, Phil had heard and read about dogs "snapping" and hurting someone, usually a small child.

He stood with Benny at the bottom of the staircase by Mary's body. Her throat was gone, the front of her nightgown a waterfall of blood, now stilled and turning black.

He reached down and clipped the leash onto Benny's collar.

Benny met his gaze and looked down with the expression of a soldier facing the results of his bullets. But a soldier can be comforted by the fact that terrible things happen in war, and that it isn't specifically his fault. This sort of comfort wasn't there for Benny and Phil.

This wasn't a war.

He turned and closed the front door, aware of the growing groups of children massing across the street in the Rosales's front yard. Some appeared to be conferring with one another, others just glared at him and Benny with some kind of hate that Phil couldn't fathom. This might not be a war, but this was going to be a siege, and for whatever reason, Scotty was the prize.

He turned back to the dead child on the floor and the tears came. He'd seen this little girl and her sisters a lot over the last year. He didn't know them well, but they were sweet little kids that chased butterflies and raced their bikes up and down the street. Mary had a pink bike and had just gotten her training wheels off. She was the youngest of the three.

Phil and Casey had gone over to their house one time for a barbecue, before Casey left him. Mary's parents, Felix and Rhonda, were lovely people, exactly the sort of people that he would have loved for him and Casey to grow up to be. Maybe that's what their problem was: too much growing up too quickly for two people that had done everything in their power to remain children as long as they could. Austin was full of people like him. He'd come to laughingly refer to it as Peter Pan Central. Now it didn't seem funny anymore. It seemed pathetic.

Mary Rosales is dead on my staircase.

She lay on her belly, having rolled down a few stairs. Benny had probably caught her near the top; the other kids had fallen backward, but not Mary. He had killed her, quickly and bloodily.

Phil looked down to Benny. The Rosales girls loved Benny. Everybody loved Benny. He was the best dog in the world: smart, obedient, intuitive, and great with kids.

Benny had killed that kid without a second thought. Benny would never do such a thing. He wouldn't hurt a fly.

Not unless that fly deserved it.

For the first time, the enormity hit Phil. Something had taken the kids, including Scotty: something that made them violent.

Violent and evil. But, truth be told, Phil didn't actually believe in evil. He believed in stupidity. He believed in insanity. He believed in greed and dumb luck, but not *evil*. The very idea flew in the face of causality. People might do bad things, but they're not evil. They might willfully and sadistically hurt people, but they're not evil. They're just products of their environment. They've got too much nature and not enough nurture.

Now that Phil was a respectable thriller writer, he read a lot about terrorists. He could name the Islamist bad guys in every dark alley in the Middle East. He knew they did stuff of such depravity, systematic rape and ethnic cleansing, that sometimes he couldn't sleep. It kept him awake nights. Nothing about the horror fiction he used to write had done that; maybe that was why he'd never sold enough books to justify writing them in the first place. But today he'd seen evil in his own son's eyes. Something calm and patient and willing. Something old and wise and unconcerned.

He looked at his reflection in the broken glass of the windows next to the doors and knew that he was no match for it. But it had his son, and Phil was going to have to get it out of him.

Whatever it was.

CHAPTER SIX

THEY HAD BEEN CLIMBING ACROSS the roof to Scotty's room when Benny's roaring face greeted them from behind the glass. Four boys, grade-school age, in shorts and t-shirts. Little boys climbing across the roof to rescue another little boy from his punishment. Springing their grounded friend. But they weren't Scotty's friends because Scotty didn't really have friends in that sense.

Despite the outré aspect of this day, that thought still struck Phil as the cruelest cut. Benny barked out his fury but Phil looked at his son. Those boys on the roof weren't going to run off with Scotty, so he wrote them off. From the corner of his eye he watched as they jumped off the roof and emerged from behind the garage to walk back toward the group in the front.

Scotty, or the one speaking from behind Scotty's face, scowled at the floor and looked back up to Phil. "It was a poorly conceived venture."

He nodded, trying to roll with the punches. "A poorly conceived venture?"

The boy looked down at the belt holding his hands to his sides. "Have you any further need of these restraints? It would be a pity for us to palaver so bound."

Phil continued to try to process his new paradigm. "Palaver?"

Scotty smiled in a very un-Scotty-like manner. Cunning and controlled. "Indeed. That we have mutual aims, you can rest assured."

Phil looked at his savaged hand. He could see the bone of his finger, and blood still dripped freely. "I'm not untying you."

A dark cloud passed over the boy's face. "Perhaps your idiot child is accustomed to wallowing in feces, but I am not."

Phil looked away. Hearing his son described like this, and the words coming from his son's own lips, was too much. Whatever this part of the thing was, he knew instinctively that he couldn't let it see him cry. And that's what today had become: a *thing*. As if events themselves had cohered into one consciousness, a death incarnate, whose wish was to snuff out sanity before snuffing out life.

His son wasn't schizophrenic. He'd heard of spontaneous schizophrenia, cases where a seemingly normal person suddenly develops multiple personalities, even to the point where a single dominant personality appears and pushes the normal consciousness to the side. But Scotty didn't have the cognitive basis for that.

A part of Phil wished he did. Perhaps every parent of a disabled child wishes this, that their child would spontaneously repair. But this wasn't a repair, this was the emergence of a vileness…

And Scotty wasn't alone. If his son had been struck schizophrenic, then so had every other kid they'd run into today.

Gas attack.

Islamist terrorist gas attack using BZ or some other kind of mega hallucinogen.

Part of him wanted to laugh. Islamists attacking a subdivision in suburbia with mega hallucinogens? It sounded like something worthy of MSNBC or Fox News's most fevered fantasies.

Phil looked down at Benny, who'd stopped barking and simply stared out the window at the bowl of clouds enveloping this section of Blackwood Estates. Benny looked back at him, his eyes hard and alert, but intently worried about those clouds.

And everything else.

Phil, this ain't Islamists.

"Okay, boy, what in the hell are we looking at?"

Scotty, or the personality inside Scotty, cleared his throat. "Would it be too great of an inconvenience for me to gain a vantage into that which you are viewing?"

Benny looked at him when he spoke, and clearly didn't like the fact that words of this sort were coming out of Scotty's mouth. Benny knew Scotty perfectly, and knew what his vocalizations meant. He knew that these words were not Scotty's.

He put his muzzle up to Scotty's face and gave it a thorough sniffing, then inspected the rest of him. Something about Scotty's demeanor changed, softened. He exhaled loud and whispered, "Bennay."

Benny put his head on Scotty's shoulder and closed his eyes.

An odd smile crossed the boy's face, and his shoulders stiffened ever so slightly.

"Your son and this wolf share a singular bond."

Phil's eyes went from the clouds to his son and back again. Benny pulled back and eyed Scotty warily.

"He's a German Shepherd."

"A Germanic sheep hound? I have heard of such from Alsace-Lorraine."

Scotty didn't have the words *Alsace-Lorraine*.

"Can you tell me how you know the words Alsace-Lorraine?"

"Yes, it's part of the German Empire, a consequence of things going badly during the Franco-Prussian War."

Phil went back to the floor, his knees giving out on him. He cradled his head in his hands. He tried to stop, to give the appearance of strength, but to no avail.

"Your self-control in the face of these adversities is admirable."

He looked back up at his tormentor and knew that no amiable words would change the fact of what he was, even though the rational part of Phil told him that it was not real, not possible, *not even happening*. Stress and divorce and single fatherhood had taken their toll and he was now destined for…

"Bedlam. That's where I found them, that's what I delivered them from."

"What?"

"The children, the ones running amok. I need to take them in hand, we must be ready when…"

"When what?"

"When the time is upon us."

Phil looked up, directly into his eyes. "Who are you?"

A cruel laugh filled the air. "Even *in extremis* it takes them an eon to ask the right questions. Is it any wonder?"

Phil tried to steel his voice. "Tell me what you've done to my boy!"

An introspective look filled Scotty's eyes. A look that his true son would never have.

"His mind is like a hall of mirrors that no thought comes through in its entirety."

Phil's resolve was shaken by the almost perfect summation of autism. He wished his facial expressions didn't give the game away, he wished he was more like the steely protagonists of his novels. Hell, he wished he was more like Benny.

"Scotty is autistic."

Scotty's head nodded slowly, a different kind of appraisal filling his son's eyes.

"I've never heard this…euphemism. Perhaps an alienist told you this?"

"People don't use the term 'alienist' anymore."

And Phil knew on a primal level that this wasn't a spontaneous case of multiple personalities, despite the fact that he really was seeing multiple personalities in the strictest sense of the term.

It wasn't spontaneous; it was *caused*.

Something did this.

Somehow, someone else's mind had been transplanted into his son's head; this had also happened to every other little kid he'd run into this morning in Blackwood Estates. And this new personality, this other person in there, was malevolent and very, very smart.

From the expression on Scotty's face, this other persona was greatly enjoying watching Phil assemble all the parts into a cohesive whole.

Phil nodded, trying to hide his confusion. "Bedlam. Tell me what you meant when you mentioned *Bedlam*."

A sardonic light filled the boy's eyes. "Were you considering new lodgings for your son?"

Phil shouted, "NO!"

"A mound of straw and manacles for his more despairing moments?"

"Never!"

"Oh, but they all say that! They're going to care for their dullards, find a place where their limited capacities will…"

"NO!"

The sound of Phil's shouting did nothing for Benny. He lay down and closed one eye, then the other. Phil blinked his own eyes; they burned and felt crusty. He breathed in and coughed. The air had only become dryer and staler feeling. Sounds carried differently in this air, they didn't seem to ring out or sustain, as if the acoustics had changed.

Scotty (or the one inside Scotty) breathed in and out loudly. He had a different look, still appraising but focused on something other than his own malice.

"You are correct in assuming that this air is different."

Phil looked up, still smarting from *his* comments on wishing to rid himself of Scotty. "Bedlam first. What did you mean when you said that's what you delivered them from? What does that mean?"

"No, little man, you tell me. What year is it and where are we?"

Phil spoke faster than he would have, and more cleverly than he would have given himself credit for being able to do. "It's 1944 and we're in Los Alamos, New Mexico."

"We are in…*the United States of America?*"

"Yes."

"In the year 1944?"

"Yes."

A black cloud of fury passed across his face. "Imbecile. What proof have you?"

Phil smiled. "Don't go anywhere, I'll be right back."

He received a dark glare from the one behind his son's face.

When he came back he was holding an old newspaper, the *Albuquerque Journal.* He'd bought it on eBay one night when he was thoroughly drunk. The reason this paper was worth buying was that a local farmer's picture covered the front page. He was at a diner proudly displaying a trophy for a prize racehorse. Behind him, Robert Oppenheimer and Enrico Fermi were eating lunch. Just a prosaic picture, pregnant with historical irony.

He held up the picture for Scotty to see.

"You are not attired in the fashion of this man."

Phil pulled the newspaper back and looked at the man on the cover.

"I'm also not a horse farmer, I'm a writer."

"A writer?"

"Yes."

"And what do you write? Are you a journalist or a playwright?"

"A novelist."

"A talentless hack, more likely."

"The *New York Times* found me to be gritty and tense."

"What does that even mean?"

"It means that it's my turn to ask you a question."

Scotty, or the thing in Scotty, assented. "Perhaps curiosity leads me to distraction. Give me your query."

"What's your name?"

"You lack the craft to employ its use, but my name is Louis Villefort."

"You have a French name and an English accent."

"The novelists of 1944 are a perceptive gang."

Phil couldn't help it, he smiled. This personality that his autistic son had spontaneously manifested was clever, but he was tied up and only knew what Phil allowed him. He wasn't sure how, but he needed to use this to his advantage.

"Okay, Louis Villefort, why are we having this conversation?"

"I'm amused by primates."

"Yet I've got you tied up, Louis."

Villefort merely looked at him as if he'd farted.

"Okay, Louis, what's the matter with the other kids? Are they like you?"

"Like me? What am I like?"

"An anomaly of schizophrenia, easily treated with lithium."

"Schizophrenia? What a dramatic word, laden with a dreary Greek oeuvre."

"And lithium?"

"I don't think a stone will help you."

"Whatever. What the hell is wrong with you kids?"

"I opened a gateway, into the Space Between the Spaces, and we emerged here."

"Okay, Louis, who is 'we'?"

"Criminals, sodomites. The sanest of the insane of Bedlam. The ones who could be of use and were least likely to balk at the means to my ends."

"How many?"

"Many."

"You're telling me about crazy people from an insane asylum. What happened to the kids here? What happened to Scotty?"

Scotty, or Louis Villefort, sat quietly, looking around. It was apparent to Phil in that moment that he wasn't the only one fighting for composure, trying to hide his facial expressions. Louis knew some of the answers, but he was in the dark too.

"Louis, is Scotty all right?"

Louis was still lost in his thoughts. He snapped to. "Yes, yes. He's fine. Yet his mind remains an impenetrable cloud to me…"

Phil let Louis continue his train of thought.

"I am here with him, I cannot despise him. This can only be natural, in my estimation. When one enters another, they join. I cannot hate him any more than I could pour scorn on my own flesh."

"Who are you, Louis?"

"To know me, you must know desire, and I doubt you have *ever* known desire."

"I've had my fun."

"Fun. Ha! Frivolity. I would know your death for uttering this comparison if I were not so bound!"

"Desire then, Louis, tell me about that."

"I will try, but I might as well explain a cypher to a horse."

"I'm waiting."

Louis exhaled a tired and old breath, and for a moment Phil could see a mind behind his son's sweet face that saw the world without pity, that took no comfort in joy, and that always won. It didn't play by the rules nor care.

"It begins with a question that there are no words to fulfill, that in the fullness of time eclipses the mundane mind. You must see. You must feel. You must know. So you begin a quest of lifetimes. Those of us more fortunate know that others came before us and left documents of their explorations. Some are mere fumblings. Others are maps of the sublime."

Phil nodded. This wasn't going anywhere, but he knew that he was dealing with a whole new order. As of this morning, the universe was a very different, very hostile place.

Louis continued. "Those such as I are different from those such as yourself. You might fancy that you are a forward-thinking man, perhaps even a scholar. You know nothing. The cosmos is no more known to you in 1944 than it was to us in 1890."

Phil smiled. Louis had just given up a key piece of information. He'd read about this sort of thing. Sociopaths were cocky and always bragged, very often implicating themselves in the process, even if said sociopath was just a multiple personality manifestation.

"So I guess your time machine malfunctioned?"

"Time machine?"

"Yeah. You and Jules Verne got in your time machine back in 1890 and emerged in New Mexico in the present? Something like that?"

Louis Villefort knew he was being mocked. "Insect. Mollusk. Where is this time machine of yours? Did your negro servant find it? You'll notice that I am presently in the body of someone else, as are the rest of my expedition."

Phil spoke her name before even thinking. "Tawana…"

"What an imaginative name for your servant, perhaps evoking deepest, darkest Africa?"

Phil didn't say anything.

Louis continued. "Pity she won't be able to go visit the mother continent."

Phil looked at the ground as another layer of enormity collapsed upon him.

Tawana was dead. This person, or personality, or whatever he was, had killed her. He'd liked Tawana. Hell, he'd fucking loved Tawana, and she'd loved Scotty and him. Over the months it had become clearer and clearer that she'd held a candle for him, and wanted him to see her as a better person than Casey. And he had, but he'd stayed in love with Casey, probably because it was really all he knew.

But that was then, and this was now, and Tawana was dead.

Louis had killed her.

Phil looked back up to him. Even though the face of his son looked back at him, something else lived behind those eyes. *Louis Villefort* was in there with Scotty.

"We escaped from Bedlam into the Space Between the Spaces. We were supposed to have emerged outside London, but we emerged here, in this time."

Phil exhaled hard. "No time machine."

Louis shook his head. "As I stated, you know no more of the spheres than we did in our time."

"So how did you do it, Louis? Magic?"

"Your scabrous ignorance is galling. Magic. Ha! Just as you fail to understand naught but rutting with your sister you must use this word: magic."

Phil couldn't help it. He laughed. "Well, Louis, I don't have a sister, but thanks for asking."

"Your simpleton wasn't a product of incest?"

Phil's anger boiled, but what could he do? Beat his son while he was tied up?

Louis nodded knowingly. "He is my flesh…and I cannot help but feel an almost bottomless empathy for him. But know this. Just as I became one with a Servitor when crossing into the Space Between the Spaces, I have become one with Scotty. This process will eventually bring even him to illumination."

"What is that supposed to mean?"

"To cross over, one must bond with a Servitor of Yog-Sothoth, an aspect of his nature. He is the Outer Dark. In so doing, the mind becomes aware. Parts are simply washed away. Weaknesses. It will happen for him in time as well."

Phil sputtered, "What? What does that even mean?"

"It means that you should be thanking me. Not only will you be relieved of the eventuality of locking the boy away, but one day his mind will be made whole."

"You're not taking my son anywhere. You're nothing more than a psychological tumor. And I promise you, you will be cut out."

Louis smiled in amusement.

Then their tension was broken by the unmistakable sound of tires squealing and children screaming.

Benny raised his head and let out a short bark and looked to Phil.

Phil ran to the bedroom window just in time to see the white SUV tearing around the corner.

Mrs. Simmons.

How long had he been up here with his son? How long had it been since he ran through the door and found Tawana dying in the back yard? How long had Scotty been tied up?

He turned on his cell. It showed that it had only been an hour. At least the clock on it still worked. The indicator said it still had no signal from the cell tower. He glanced out across the street at the assembly of children. There had to be thirty or forty down there, standing in the Rosales's front yard, most of them staring back at him.

"You're their leader, aren't you, Louis?"

"I led them from captivity, they are my people. When they crossed over and bonded with the Servitors, their madnesses were diminished and they became more than they were."

Phil looked down at Benny and a terrible chill went up his spine. "They were trying to get to you. One of them is dead."

"Your animal will pay for this. It is up to you to decide whether you pay with him."

Phil wrinkled his nose and shuddered. There was a dead little girl laying on his staircase, but he felt more for Benny than he did for her. That little girl had parents who loved her as much as he loved Scotty.

Were they home? Was he supposed to go tell them? How does that sort of thing even work?

He walked out of Scotty's room and peered down. There really was a dead little girl laying crumpled and pathetic on his staircase. His hand went to his mouth and his eyes bulged in horror. He didn't know if he should cry or vomit. He slowly and carefully walked to her and reached down to check her neck for a pulse. Nothing. Her skin was turning a startling blue and the smell of blood was overpowering. Thick, meaty, and rusty, but the unreal dryness of the air rendered it sharper, dustier.

The windows next to the door and in the living room and dining room to his left and right were broken out, and little children's faces sneaked peeks over bushes and around windowsills. Children's faces, but not children's facial expressions.

Hard, cold, gleefully sadistic.

They wanted to kill him and Benny, and he was sure they would relish every second. They seemed to have some sort of preternatural hatred for Benny.

He walked quickly back up to Scotty's room.

"Okay, Louis…"

But it wasn't Louis, it was Scotty this time, Benny gently nuzzling his face. He was crying softly.

Phil's eyes glassed with tears, soothing the dryness setting in. "Scotty?"

Scotty smiled at him. Scotty's smile. Guileless, pure innocence.

"Ba-baaaa roo?"

This was how Scotty said "bathroom." He wanted to go to the bathroom. About a year ago he'd stopped needing a diaper, but it wasn't wise to push it.

Scotty smiled expectantly. "Ba-baaaa roo?"

Phil nodded and did his best to look happy. Scotty was absolutely empathetic. If you were happy, then he was happy. Sadness and anger worked the same way. He had enough to deal with being confused and frightened by the world around him. He didn't need anyone's negativity compounding that.

Phil carefully approached him and loosened the belt holding his arms to his sides, leaving the makeshift bonds tied around his ankles. Scotty happily held his arms up to be carried. Phil made an exaggerated face and held his hands to his back, indicating that his back hurt and he couldn't carry Scotty, but instead went around him and hugged him from the back and picked him up by the shoulders to stand him up on his feet.

Scotty took a few hesitant steps with the bonds around his ankles and Phil made a happy face. *This is a game; let's both walk in little steps to the bathroom.* Scotty smiled. He liked games.

Benny stood at his side and licked his hand.

Scotty giggled. "Bennay!"

And they walked to the bathroom.

Phil sat on the side of the bathtub and Scotty merrily pooped. Phil made sure to smile and laugh, to keep Scotty's mood in place. Benny stood in the doorway and wagged his tail happily. He knew this game.

Occasionally he looked over his shoulder, then to Phil.

All clear for now, Phil. They are still outside, but they're in the yard.

Phil nodded and turned his attention back to Scotty.

After he'd helped Scotty wipe and gotten his pants back up, he had to think hard about what to do next. Louis Villefort was the most complex manifestation of multiple personality schizophrenia he'd ever heard of. He'd read lots of horror novels where this affliction played a major role, but he knew that in reality it was far less functional than popular fiction led on.

Louis Villefort shouldn't be possible. The kids outside shouldn't be possible.

The weather was possible, just rather improbable.

And those clouds, they didn't make any sense whatsoever.

Suddenly there was a sound, a trumpeting like a whale or an elephant. It wasn't close, but it wasn't that far away either. Scotty's expression became clear and hard again; Louis was back and he looked terrified. He took two steps running toward the bedroom door and was tackled by

Benny. Gently, but not too gently. Benny pinned him by the shoulders and stood above him in a show of pure pack dominance. There was no mistaking who was in charge.

Louis' eyes were wild. "Accursed wolf! You will die for—"

Then he stopped talking. The trumpeting call came again, this time from another direction. He took a deep breath and looked around the room, knowing he had panicked, knowing that he had shown a fearful face when he shouldn't have. He looked up to Phil, his eyes narrowing in appraisal. Could this man from 1944 understand what had frightened him?

"Louis? What in the flying fuck was that?"

Louis swallowed and held up his hands, showing Benny and Phil that he was going to stop struggling.

"I'm not certain what manner…what *order* of thing made that sound."

Phil shook his head. "Sounds. Plural. One came from that direction, I think." He pointed out the bedroom window. "And it sounds like something responded from another direction. There were two of them."

"Nothing could have followed us through…" Louis was speaking to himself, but he looked uncertain, and didn't have a response to the statement he had made.

Phil had never heard a noise like that before, and something about its sheer power told him that it wasn't from here, whatever that meant.

Louis, and those kids, and the clouds. Not from here either.

He knelt down next to Louis and Benny. "Followed you through from where, Louis? What the hell does that mean?"

Louis held up Scotty's hand in front of his face and looked at it in amazement, as if seeing it for the first time. He slowly sat up, his body language telling Benny that he would neither fight nor flee, and turned to look into the little mirror on the wall. Surely he'd seen his—Scotty's — reflection in the bathroom, if not before. But he looked at it with both fear and wonderment.

He turned to Phil with an odd sort of determination. "This one knows nothing of New Mexico in 1944. *Nothing at all.* But I know this, at least: those sounds were certainly not from New Mexico in 1944."

He stopped for a moment, absorbed in thought. "May I look out the window at those clouds, please?"

CHAPTER SEVEN

IT WAS UNFAIR BY ANY approximation, but Phil had Louis strapped in the child seat with the belt restraining his arms to his sides. Louis snarled at him when he put the belt around him; he knew he couldn't escape Phil, and certainly not Benny. Phil even added insult to injury by strapping his bike helmet on his head.

Then he and Benny got into the green Ford Explorer and Phil cursed as he forgot that the automatic garage door opener wouldn't function in the absence of electricity. He warily walked over to the door and heaved it up, catching four kids, or whatever they were now, glaring at him from halfway up his driveway.

He put it in gear and pulled out, the crowd of children pulling back away, as if they were frightened of automobiles, as if they'd never seen them before. Louis maintained a stoic but angry expression on his face. It appeared that the children across the street couldn't see him in the truck.

As soon as the Explorer was out of the driveway, all of the children sprinted, screaming wildly, into Phil's house. He could hear them screaming from inside even as he pulled away. Screaming, arms waving, in some kind of default mental mode that was neither them nor the personality besetting them.

"Looks like your pals were pretty excited about seeing you. Sorry to say, but they're in for a bit of disappointment."

He grinned into the rearview mirror at Louis glaring back at him, Benny sitting next to him fixing him with a hard stare of knowing.

They slowly rolled past Lloyd's house with its waist-high white picket fence and explosion of garish flowers in the front yard. The Home Owners' Association had tried to fight him on this, but Lloyd was a lawyer. A creepy lawyer with in-your-face liberal politics hiding a deep vein of perversion. Lloyd might claim to be a put-upon gay man, the defender of all the put-upon of the world, but his leer told otherwise. He wasn't into anything as vanilla as gay sex between consenting adults.

Or so Phil suspected… But Phil was well-aware of the limits of his own understanding of the real world. He'd tried hard as a younger man to know the weird fringe grey areas, but he knew all of this from research, not from any kind of true experience. He was really kind of a boring guy. So Lloyd's kinks were really a great big question mark to him. He'd never been into anything transgressive, even anything risqué.

Lloyd's house seemed untouched by this children's mutiny.

Other houses weren't. As Phil rolled slowly by and his own house was in the rearview mirror, he observed that about every third house had at least one broken window on the first floor. One house had a ladder leading up to the second floor and a broken window there. Blackwood Estates was a still, quiet place by day, but never motionless. Today, however, it was. Either all of the predacious children were gathered around his home, or they slinked about, stealthy as cats hunting birds.

He passed Mrs. Simmons's street and turned to look down to her house and the subdivision's end. Whether her white SUV was there or not, he couldn't tell.

He continued past the stop sign down his street to where the big curve began. He could see from this approach that it looked like the big dome of clouds touched down around that curve and several blocks down, this end of the subdivision coming closest to Parmer and the roller rink.

What was beyond that?

Fog?

Suddenly Phil realized that he wasn't even sure if that was how fog worked, or how clouds worked for that matter. Is fog just what you call a cloud when it touches the ground? Or are they separate phenomena? He glanced back in the mirror at Louis and Benny. Did they know how little he really knew about anything? Or that maybe he'd be best described as a lucky loser?

He passed through the aisle of suburban architectural confections, perfect lawns, and gleaming white driveways and around the corner. He could see the place where the ground met the sky a few blocks on. He slowed as he neared, amazed by the starkness.

***

As Phil stopped the truck, Louis gave a cry as if being tormented with fire, and Benny let out a sympathetic whine of agreement. This place, this juncture, was wrong, just fundamentally wrong.

There was a hiss, like the sigh of a beer can, as Phil opened the door. He felt the air rush out of the car. The atmosphere in the car, recirculated on the way over from his house, was noticeably different closer to this juncture.

The air was even dryer over here.

The clouds touched the ground. At least, that's what it looked like. A trick of dry ice and stage craft, just on a cyclopean scale. A wall of cloud going straight up to where the uniformity of its greyness became indistinguishable from anything around it. Only from a distance could you see that it went far above the roofs of the houses, but the greyness gave no sense of depth. How high it went was unknowable without some other kind of aid.

And Phil didn't have that aid.

He closed the car door and the caterwauling of Louis and Benny ceased, becoming just a dull noise in the background. The hairs on his arms and face felt the very distinct prickle of static electricity, as if it were slowly but surely growing in strength. The air was creating a perfect fusion of hot and dry to create dry lightning. He stepped forward to the face of the clouds. Just clouds, but also a boundary, a visible manifestation of the tension between what was on this side and what lay on the other.

He listened closely. No sound of wind, even though there was an ever-so-slight current of air moving toward the cloud face. A scared thought hit Phil. *What I'm feeling is the moisture getting sucked right out of the air. These clouds aren't from the other side, whatever that is, they're from this side. This is the water being pulled out from all sides, and pressed up against something else, holding it in, or only slowly letting it out.*

He filtered out all the sounds from around him, even though there were ominously few. No background chatter of birds and squirrels, no underlying hum of insects. He even filtered out the sound of Benny and Louis howling in the car.

And then he heard it.

Waves, the soft lap of waves against a shore. The more he focused, the bigger it sounded. Just a few feet on the other side of the curtain of clouds was a vast body of water. He began to take a step forward, wanting to see with his own eyes this new and bizarre facet to the puzzle, when he was stopped by an uptick of noise from the car. Benny was barking furiously, his face pressed against the windshield, paws buffeting against the glass.

Come back, don't go in there, Phil!

He turned his head to regard Benny and caught a glimpse of Scotty in the background. It wasn't Louis, it was Scotty, and he was having an episode, banging his head against the side of the car seat, going at it with every ounce of strength he could muster.

Phil was by his side at the open rear passenger door in a second, grateful that he'd made Louis wear the bicycle helmet. If he hadn't, Scotty would have been a bruised and bloody mess. Phil's hands flew over the straps holding Scotty in the car seat, yanking him out and into the grass next to his truck. He rolled him on his stomach and lifted him up to clear his airway and prevent Scotty from choking to death.

Benny bounded around in excited circles, looking outward and wary, but maintaining silence. His training was very deliberate about his raising an alert.

Then Scotty vomited and Benny screamed like he was being shot. Scotty's vomit hit the ground, and more and more followed it, a noxious stream. But the forming pile moved, wriggling and writhing, covered in digestive slime.

Baby birds.

Blind and naked.

Phil screamed and Scotty choked out load after noisome load. Benny continued screeching. Phil had never heard Benny in any kind of fury like this before. He'd only seen this in a dog that had been run over on the highway.

Finally the purging was done, and a pile of dying baby birds lay in front of them. Phil cradled Scotty, who was still trying to catch his breath.

But it was Louis who emerged, gasping, from inside Scotty's skin. "Phil! Take me away now, that was just the first tremor before it breaks free! We are too close to this Erasure, it comes! We must away, now, now, sir!"

A shiver of disgust and existential revulsion passed through Phil. He'd never had one of those before today either.

***

Inside the truck, Louis continued to moan, but sometimes it was Scotty. This close to the clouds, Louis seemed to lose his sure control.

Phil jingled the keys as he struggled to get his shaking hands to cooperate. Louis and Benny were right, each in their own way. This place was wrong. This borderland next to the cloud face was volatile. He could feel it in every fiber of his being. And it was getting much worse by the second. Something was approaching this place from the other side.

Phil's hands stopped shaking. He looked to his sides and around to the back. The sky was dark. But it wasn't because of the clouds; it was because the sun was almost all the way down. Sunset was at almost 9 PM this late in the summer.

Another wave of vertigo hit Phil. "Louis, does time work differently near this fucking thing?"

Louis coughed and spat out a line of gummy mucus. "Fool, get us gone! This is no mere border; this is an Erasure!"

Phil spun back around and continued to fumble with the keys. The clouds in front of him started to ripple, as if agitated from behind. They weren't rippling elsewhere. Something knew they were here. Something was approaching. From behind the clouds, a symmetrical constellation of lights mirrored left and right, like a whale-sized luminescent deep sea fish had come to press itself on the bowl, but from the outside.

Louis screamed, "God, man, get us clear!"

Phil stomped on the gas and his truck's tires screeched out their response. He took them a block in reverse, then slammed on the brakes and swung the back of the truck over the curb and up onto a neighbor's lawn. He cut the wheel the other way and threw it into gear, putting the full weight of his foot to the floor and tearing down the next two blocks to Mrs. Simmons's intersection.

He hit the brakes, coming to a dead halt.

Mrs. Simmons sat in her white Escalade, and Prius Latina in Reflector Shades Listening to Metallica and her husband sat in her back seat. Phil rolled his window down and she rolled hers down. Her normally fine face was a smear of makeup, tears, and sweat. She had a big bruise on her forearm and a jagged scrape across the left side of her face. That would leave a scar.

Her eyes were wide with confusion and panic. "Are you seeing this shit too?"

CHAPTER EIGHT

EVERYTHING ABOUT JAYNE SIMMONS'S HOUSE was as
Phil expected it to be.

Tastefully, contemplatively beige.

Too big, too tastefully furnished, too polished, too quiet. This was
a place where hope came to die after dreams were shown to be nothing
more than dreams. A prison masquerading as a life, perfect if you can
manage to never think about it.

Sort of like his own life, just more stereotypically so.

Her daughter, Wendy, was nowhere to be found. Jayne drove off
after her child attacked her, then came back and found she was gone.
She'd run into Esme Salazar (Prius Latina in Reflector Shades Listening to
Metallica) and her husband, Rick. They'd pulled up at his house to gawk
because the mob of kids were "screaming and rioting." They got out of
Esme's Prius to yell at the kids, and Rick had a puncture wound through
his left hand to show for it. A kid had stabbed him with a Mont Blanc
fountain pen, looted from Phil's own house. It had been a gift from Casey
right after he signed his publishing contract, right before the money
changed her moral DNA.

Jayne pulled up in her Escalade and they jumped in her back seat.

They were in shock, they were confused, they were like him.

Esme was bandaging Rick's hand while he wept softly. He didn't look
like a weepy kind of guy, but what he'd been through was so sudden, and
so off the charts. If crying was his way of venting, Phil could respect him
for that. At least he wasn't screaming or being violent.

Scotty, or Louis, killed Tawana this morning.

Phil winced in painful regret. He sat on the couch, shaking his head
and looking at the floor. One afternoon last winter, Scotty had been down
with the flu and had slept all day. Phil and Tawana had ended up just
talking all morning. Then one thing had led to another, and it had been
really good, but he hadn't ever even previously considered that something

like that could happen. Yes, Tawana was cute, but he was a nerdy white guy and didn't know anything outside of that.

As soon as he'd pulled out and looked at her hungry eyes, he realized that she liked him, she really liked him. She'd liked him for a while, but he'd never considered her because of her color and her culture. He didn't even know that about himself until the deed was done.

He'd never given her a chance, and now she was dead.

The next day he told her it couldn't happen again, that he was still too hung up on Casey. While that was true, he knew that underneath it lay a less palatable reason, one he'd never allowed himself to look at squarely. But now…there was no avoiding it. He didn't have the tears that Rick had, but he wished he did for being such a fool.

"So what happened next?" Esme's voice snapped Phil back to the present.

Benny killed a kid.

Phil's eyes shifted to the door of the next room where Benny watched Scotty, or Louis, whichever one he was right now.

"He bit me, and then…then the kids started screaming from outside and he screamed back. It was fucking freaky, it didn't sound human, more like a…a bird or a whale or something."

He stopped and exhaled hard.

"He was answering them, like hyenas calling to one another. Then they attacked, and five of them charged up the stairs and…and…"

Phil's breathing went sideways, and he started having trouble getting enough air.

Jayne put her hand on his. "It's okay, take your time."

He shook his head. "They were going to kill us. Benny knew. He knows what people's intentions are and…"

Esme and Jayne looked at each other in horror.

Jayne broke the silence. "Phil, did Benny hurt one of those kids?"

Phil shook his head, not in denial, but in affirmation that Benny didn't just hurt one of those kids.

Jayne pulled back, looking through the doorway to the next room where Benny stood guard. "Phil, what color hair did that little girl have?"

Phil's eyes grew wide as he understood her real question. *Did your dog kill my daughter?*

Phil shook his head. "No, no, it wasn't her. It wasn't your daughter."

It was someone else's daughter.

Part of Jayne's expression revealed relief, but not most of it. Her daughter had tried to kill her this morning, and in a panic she escaped in her Escalade. Phil had watched this happen. But when Jayne came back to try to find her, she was gone.

Rick shook his head and winced. "Phil, what's behind those clouds?"

Benny appeared in the doorway and gave a short bark, then turned to face the front door and gave a low growl. *Phil, we got company.*

Phil leapt up from the couch and ran into the bedroom where Scotty/Louis lay tied on the bed. He glanced at the windows and saw forms skulking through the shadows of Jayne's back yard. He picked up Scotty, who was kicking and cursing and clearly now Louis, and carried him into the living room.

He dropped Louis on the couch and looked around the room. It was dark, past sunset, and they saw by view of candlelight. Jayne had lit several, but these were decorative, not meant for serious illumination.

"Jayne, we need more light. Rick, are you okay? They're gonna make their move soon."

Rick just nodded his head. "Yeah."

Esme shook her head. "What? What's that supposed to mean? 'Make their move'?"

Jayne started going through a cabinet, pulling out boxes of candles. Martha Stewart to the fucking rescue. She started lining the mantle and tables, lighting them as she went.

Phil looked around the room. He'd never thought about it, but practically every external surface was a fucking window. When these kids attack...

Louis answered his question for him. "Let me go, and you will go unharmed."

Esme stuttered. "What? What is going on?"

Something slammed into the door and there was a sound of screaming. Unhinged, pure insanity screaming. There were probably fifty of them on the front lawn. Then silence, then another scream. Not a child this time, but an adult woman in terror and agony.

Phil pointed to Louis. "Take him upstairs and watch him. Rick, let's go."

As Esme and Jayne lugged a snarling Louis up the stairs, Phil, Rick, and Benny huddled at the front door. Through the eyehole they could see the crowd. They were carrying torches like a medieval mob of peasants come to storm the tower.

Luckily they're too small to wield pitchforks, Phil thought.

Then he glanced at the bandage on his hand and the one on Rick's, and thought the better of it.

He glanced from Rick to Benny. "We're gonna just go out on the porch, see if...well, see what we're really up against."

Rick handed him a golf club, while he held a mop handle. He looked petrified.

"Phil, don't let them get close. They will fucking kill you. The only reason that pen didn't go through my throat was that my hand was in the way."

Phil nodded. "Benny, you ready? Don't let them hurt you, boy."

Benny looked back. *I'm here to protect you, not the other way around.*

They stepped back and Rick pulled the door open quickly. The torchlit night framed the faces of children, eyes rolled back, teeth bared, *screaming.* A single high-pitched note, wavering then recovering, sustained for longer than should have been possible.

Then they stopped. No signal, no command given, they just stopped.

And gazed at their targets with hunger in their eyes.

The twins, Denny and Penny, stepped forward from the mob, dirty and disheveled, but their smiles were still razors. Penny spoke, her words belying the youth of her voice. "We have come to parley for Louis Villefort. You will give him to us, and we will pass from this place. You will be unharmed."

Rick shook his head. "How the fuck do you know what this kid's schizo alter ego is named?"

And under his breath: "How do they know that, Phil?"

Phil was slow in getting a handle on what was being said. A mob of kids with the same complex as his son was demanding that he be allowed to join them and...

He stopped his mind from becoming a tornado, winds bearing impossibilities instead of lethal fragments. Phil held up a hand and shook his head. Benny let out a growl and a fierce sounding bark to second the motion.

"What is your name? Or, rather, what do you think your name is?"

Penny, or the thing inside of Penny, laughed. "And what could you do with that?"

Rick shook his head and scoffed. "What are you, a fucking lawyer? Fuck you, kid."

It seemed impossible that Penny's smile could grow brighter and harder, but it did. "I've fucked a thousand men and the constabulary locked me away for it. Perhaps you've brought a few shillings to get your wand waxed, my lord?"

The entire assembly of children laughed in cynical agreement.

Rick looked to Phil with an amazed dismay. Even though these kids had tried to kill him today, he still was out to sea.

Phil wasn't faring any better. "You don't scare us, and this batshit crazy act is…"

Penny's hand went to her face and she spat into her hand, a big black wad of filth. Benny let out a strained yelp like he'd just been hit with an electrical shock, and he backed up two steps.

The wad of slime in Penny's hand began to move. She inverted her palm and it dripped down from her hand, pulsating as the strands elongated, forming into the shape of a nauseous black worm that sprouted centipede-like legs when it touched the ground and ran off into the brush. It was at least a foot long.

Rick whimpered. "Jesus. Jesus fucking Christ!"

Phil gasped but said nothing. He hadn't told his new colleagues anything about what he'd seen at the cloud border, nothing about the impossible pile of writhing baby birds that his son had vomited forth.

Penny looked up from her hand, up from the trail of slime that the worm/centipede abomination left in its wake. "Many things have come to pass that were not foreseen. Villefort alone knows the secret paths. *Lorsque les étoiles s'alignent, nous ouvrirons une porte sur l'espace entre les espaces.*"

Phil gasped. Villefort had said this same thing to him earlier. "What does that mean? Tell me what the fuck that means!"

Penny shook her head. "My name is Elizabeth Cromwell, but I'm no lord. I'm his whore, his Magdalene." She looked around her assembly and then back to Phil. "He saved us all from Bedlam. Now we will save him from you."

This was some sort of signal to the rest, because those in the back handed an array of shovels, hoes, pool sticks, and other long-handled tools through to the front, forming them into a phalanx that may have been comical if it were not for the deadly intent in the children's faces. She shook her head and laughed.

"Oh, ye of little faith! Do not doubt our resolve. Before we are done you will give over the wolf as well."

Phil didn't understand this exchange one bit, but he pulled the leash from his side pocket and quickly clipped it to Benny's collar.

Benny looked up to him with wide eyes. *Phil, something really fucked up is about to go down.*

Phil whispered, "Whatever happens, stick together, don't let them…"

The crowd parted down the middle and four kids pushed forward a wheelbarrow with the pitiful cargo of a Mexican woman in a maid's uniform. She was tied to it with a cruel arrangement of electrical cords and Christmas lights. She was bruised and battered and filthy. There was a gag in her mouth, and she looked to Phil and Rick with pleading eyes.

And then a single hoe fell down on her head, penetrating her skull.

54

Rick screamed. "*Ay dios mio!*"

A second hoe fell on her head, digging through hair and skin and bone. The woman's body convulsed and her eyes bulged. The wielders of the hoes yanked back, pulling her head apart. Her motions stilled and her brain fell to the ground, emptying her ruined head.

Rick was on his knees, still chanting, "*Ay dios mio, ay dios mio!*"

Phil was next to him, trying to pull the man to his feet.

Then the butchering began, and the children fed.

Benny pulled Phil, and Phil pulled Rick, back into the house.

As they closed the door behind them to hide from the bloody bacchanal, they heard Penny/Elizabeth Cromwell's voice mocking them from behind. "How many more scared little hares will we find hiding in these homes? We will bring them forth, one at a time, until you give us Louis Villefort!"

CHAPTER NINE

J AYNE AND ESME WATCHED THE whole thing from windows on the second floor.

They held each other, sobbing and traumatized. Most people have never seen a person die, much less brutally murdered, then torn into by children more hyena than human.

From behind them, Louis Villefort assessed and judged quietly.

Esme whispered prayers in Spanish and Jayne cradled her. She was a mother and that's what she knew to do. Esme and Rick had waited to have children, and Esme had no comfort in the ability to comfort another, a cruel form of suffering in and of itself.

Jayne, on the other hand, was a mother, and lived not just with the fear of the things she had witnessed, but also that her daughter had been taken by this malignance and she had failed to protect her.

They were both adrift in a world that was showing a face that until now was impossible.

When Jayne heard the pounding on the bedroom door, she quietly disentangled herself from the quaking Esme and let in Phil and Rick and Benny. Rick went to Esme and they folded in on one another, sobbing until their faces were red from the strain.

Phil looked to Jayne. "Are you okay?"

She screamed back, "How in the fuck would I be okay?"

His own hands were shaking and he felt as if he could easily vomit, but he was in much better shape than any of them, save for Benny.

He whispered, "I'm sorry, I'm so sorry."

Louis smiled and laughed.

And then the sound came back. Like an air raid siren combined with a whale song, a sound that wasn't from here.

The smile dropped from Louis' face.

Jayne looked around bewildered. "What the hell is that? It's that same sound from earlier."

Phil's reticence to take a leap into the unknown had been shattered by the intrusion of the unknown. "Louis, what the fuck is that noise?"

Almost as soon as the unreal trumpeting ceased there was a shouting from outside. Not a screaming, as was these children's wont, but a panicked shouting. Phil quickly stepped over and parted the shades to see the kids scattering in all directions, a general rout. Their grisly supper was left in bits and pieces across the carefully manicured lawn of Jayne Simmons.

Another of the long trumpeting blasts echoed out of the night, and just as before it came from the opposite direction of the first, an elephantine response. Something out there was answering something else out there.

No one spoke, and all eyes were on Phil as he watched the scores of children melt away into the night, sprinting as fast as their tiny legs would carry them. Whatever these sounds were, the kids wanted no part of whatever made them.

Phil closed the blinds and turned back to everyone in the room. "Louis, what was that thing behind the clouds?"

Louis' face gave away his genuine fear and confusion. He looked from face to face, but his bravado slipped ever-so-slightly. "There are consequences for every exploration, and rents are paid in flesh."

Rick whispered, "What the fuck is that supposed to mean?"

Esme whispered, "You fucking little monster."

Jayne whispered, "Yeah."

Phil joined in. "Why the fuck are we all whispering now?"

Louis answered him. "Because the Hunters of the Outer Dark have found this place."

Esme whimpered and tugged on Rick's shirt. "Let's go, baby, let's go home and close the door. We'll go to bed and when we wake up this will all be over..."

Rick stroked her hair and looked into her eyes. "Shhh, baby, we're safer here with friends."

Esme pulled back from him and raised her voice, pointing at Louis. "Is that what you call a friend? It's a fucking demon in a little boy!"

Louis smirked at them. "Very touching, but silence your woman, Indian. We lack the time for hysterical women."

Rick hissed back, "Shut your fuckhole, *puto*."

Benny let out a dismayed whine. This was going sideways.

Phil raised his hands. "Rick, Esme... It's not a demon, it's..." And he trailed off.

Jayne shook her head. "It's what, Phil?"

Phil swallowed hard, painful in the drying air. "From his accent I'd say he's from London in the late 1800's…" He trailed off, exhaled hard, and started again. "Scotty is autistic. There's no human way that he could…that he could speak this way. He can only speak in simple words and gestures."

Louis shook his head. "Bravo. We call upon the author to explain!"

Esme looked at Phil hard. "*Pinche loco gabacho.*"

Rick shook his head. "Esme, we gotta figure this out, even if we start with crazy."

Jayne looked at the floor. "I heard about Scotty from Lloyd Reynolds. I didn't know he's autistic. He told me Scotty was…retarded."

Even after all that he'd seen today, hearing that still burned Phil up. "That stupid bigoted fuck."

Jayne looked up from the floor and sobbed. "Wendy wasn't Wendy anymore. She was someone else. She spoke like that little girl on the lawn, and like i." She gestured to Louis. "Wendy wouldn't know Victorian English from Greek. She's a little girl and she sure as shit doesn't know Latin either. But she said some things in Latin. And the screaming, it was like…"

Rick prodded. "Like what, Jayne?"

She nodded as if reaching an agreement with herself. "Just like those other kids. It's like some kind of… It's like they go into this brain shutdown mode and…"

But she didn't need to explain, they'd all seen it firsthand.

Esme didn't buy it. She looked at Louis. "Okay, where you from, *ese?*"

Louis smiled. "The patois of Mexico is fascinating."

Esme shook her head, pissed. "I'm not Mexican, I'm a fucking American, asshole."

There was a sound like the groaning of enormous metal springs, a creaking high and impossibly low. Louis' face lost all trace of mockery and his eyes went wide. His head jerked toward the window and back to Phil.

"It comes! Quickly! You must silence me if I…if your son cries out, and he will cry out. Just as at the cloud face, I will lose control, and your son will return, in terror. You must silence him and all of them or it will devour us!"

Then came the sound of footsteps, a low and thunderous sound, like a parade of elephants grown to the size of whales, or an elephant with twenty, thirty, forty legs. Then it roared and trumpeted, a whale song to tear the firmament.

And again, the same sound came, but from the other direction.

Two of them, coming from opposite sides of the cloud border imprisoning Blackwood Estates. Two of them, whatever they were.

Jayne was at the window, peeking through the blinds. Her breath caught and released in short bursts. Her hands shook and the blinds rattled. She pulled away gasping and retching.

Phil stood quickly and peeked though. "Oh, Jesus fucking fuck."

There were no lights, so the subdivision was darker than usual, but *it* was darker still. If anything could describe it, it would be that it was Darkness itself. Blacker than the blackness around it, seeming to draw what glimmers of light existed right from the air around it. It was Darkness, but it was luminous, with a constellation of nodes that glowed but illuminated nothing.

And the more Phil looked, the more he saw.

He saw Casey doing a line of cocaine in a bar bathroom, then sucking a man's cock who punched her in the face repeatedly. He saw Scotty in a filthy institution, burned by sadistic wardens, forced to eat feces. He saw a man force-feeding Jayne fish hooks, one after another. He saw in the end that in each of these waking nightmares, he himself was the one inflicting the torment. He was the abuser; he was the sadist.

Jayne pulled him hard away from the window and he fell to the floor gasping for air, tears pouring from his burning dry eyes. He shouted, "God!"

And Jayne's hand covered his mouth.

Louis hissed. "Yes, silence him! It will deceive your mind until you scream in delirium, in your madness you will not be able to escape and it will devour you, body and soul!"

Jayne held her hand covering his mouth until his terrified eyes registered recognition again. She released him, but the tears still flowed from both of their eyes.

She said, "I saw it too. I saw it. I saw hell."

Louis' head jerked back and forth and he began to choke. "Philip, restrain me! Now, fool!"

And he was Scotty again. Scotty, having a seizure, screaming.

Phil grabbed him. He put his hand over Scotty's mouth, and held it there until he stopped moving, rendered unconscious by lack of oxygen to the brain. As Scotty's body went limp, Phil's tears, his guilt, his failure, was complete. Jayne put a hand over his, her tears pouring down her face. She cried for a father forced to do such a terrible thing to save a defenseless child.

Esme began digging in her purse, talking to herself. "I'm not looking at it, I'm not looking at it, it's gonna be okay…"

She pulled out a compact mirror and ran to the window, standing to the side. She held the blinds apart and the mirror at arm's length, angling it to look outside, but by reflection only.

"Holy fucking God! It's...it's...it's like a black cloud full of stars...but it's a spider and a...squid and teeth and eyes with gears and aborted..."

She dropped the mirror and pressed her back against the wall next to the window.

Rick sat on the floor staring at his wife, immobilized by the chaos of the last few moments. "What was it, what did you see?"

Esme whispered, "It's as big as a house, and it's walking down the middle of the street and it's coming this way and there's another one out there too. It's looking for us."

Rick asked again, "What was it? What did you see?"

She looked from face to face in the room around her. "I think God is dead."

Rick stood slowly and deliberately and went to his wife. He held her face in his hands and kissed her gently on the cheek and shook his head. "I'm not going to look out that window because I know what's out there. It's just a mirror. It shows you what your mind can't handle. It's just like a chameleon. It shows you things that aren't really there."

Then they heard a scream from a house somewhere down the street.

The scream of a child, the plaintive scream of an ordinary child being devoured by nightmares manifested into the real world. The Hunter had found his first prey of the night. Then from the other direction, the foghorn whale song blared out of the night again, and there was the sound of breaking glass and splintering beams. A house was being torn open to pry out the helpless victims inside. A trio of children's shrieks, then silence.

It went on and on until light filtered back through the blinds. That night they stayed in Jayne's walk-in closet. Rick held Esme and Phil held Scotty. Jayne held herself. They closed their eyes, but they didn't sleep.

CHAPTER TEN

"THERE'S NO WATER." JAYNE TURNED the knobs on the faucet, and the pipes made a protesting sound throughout the house, but the water only trickled, then stopped entirely.

Phil was about to attempt to explain this rather obvious thing, but Jayne held up a hand and shook her head. *I'm in no mood, dipshit.*

Phil wanted to say something comforting but thought better of it. Maybe a woman with a missing and presumably possessed daughter didn't want to hear any platitudes from a beta male whose best friend is a dog.

Right now, Scotty was Scotty. He smiled bashfully at all the new people around him. Rick smiled back; Esme and Jayne weren't ready for any smiles. Benny was practically in heaven. He kept putting his head on Scotty's shoulder and closing his eyes, savoring the moment and saying a silent prayer. *Scotty, Scotty, please stay Scotty, please don't let that thing take over my beloved friend.*

Esme closed her eyes and rubbed her face. "My fucking eyes are killing me. What the fuck is wrong with the god damn air?"

Something like a smile passed over Jayne's face and she walked out of the bathroom to hand Esme a bottle of eye drops.

Esme nodded appreciatively. "Hell yeah, that's what I'm talking about."

Esme handed the bottle down to Rick and turned to Phil. "You need to tell us what the fuck you saw at the edge of the clouds."

Phil nodded his head, but was beginning to wonder about Esme. She seemed to be losing it, and the last thing they needed in a crazy situation was a crazy person.

"Well, Louis said that he wanted to see the clouds and…"

Esme shook her head rapidly, her face in a grimace. "No. His fucking name is Scotty and this is just fucking…schizo shit, man, multiple personality shit!"

Phil couldn't look at her. She seemed pretty damn close to the edge;

challenging her now could push her over. And despite the fact that she was basically advocating for a sane and rational explanation, they'd both seen the thing that walked their streets last night, and they'd both seen Penny, or Elizabeth Cromwell, spit out a blob of slime that transformed into a worm and then into an impossible centipede thing. They were in uncharted waters, and denying that was possibly the truest act of insanity.

Phil cleared his throat and tried to speak as calmly as he could. "We got to the cloud face and I got out of my truck. It made a noise like opening a beer can or something, the air just rushed out. It's getting pulled out toward the edges. I don't think the air is escaping, but the water in the air seems to be. It like we're being dried out…"

Esme interrupted. "So the water is getting sucked out of the air by whatever is on the other side of those clouds."

It didn't sound like a question, it was more of a statement.

"Those clouds are the water vapor, like they're pressed up against something, some kind of barrier."

Rick looked up from the floor. "It's a circle, we're inside a circle."

Phil shook his head. "I think it's more like a bowl."

And then Louis was back. Maybe he'd been back for a few moments, maybe he was watching the whole time, a passive observer behind Scotty's guileless eyes.

"I believe a sphere is the most apropos descriptor, the bottom extending far into the ground," he said, his usual laconic smile absent.

Esme snarled. "Shut the fuck up."

Louis' smile still didn't return. "I, *we*, Phil, do not have time to bandy words with your fool Indian woman."

Esme was quick, but Benny was quicker. She lunged at Scotty, eyes on fire, arms extended, but was intercepted by a mouthful of fangs. It was over in seconds. He didn't break the skin, but she was flung against the bedside nightstand, knocking it over and sending the lamp crashing to the floor.

Rick jumped to her aid.

Phil jumped on Rick.

Jayne jumped on Phil.

Esme snarled and spit flew. "Him! He's the problem! It was him caused this shit! Fucking ringleader, man!"

Rick was also much quicker than he looked. He got in a fierce uppercut to Phil's chin and Phil barely held on to consciousness. When Jayne pulled Phil off of Rick, he was mostly dead weight, seeing stars.

It was over before it started, but lines had been drawn. Esme wanted to kill Louis, Rick wanted to protect his wife, Phil wanted to protect

Scotty, and Jayne wanted to stop the fighting.

The groups sat divided, Jayne holding Phil back, but mostly holding him up. Rick held Esme's shoulders. She wasn't done yet. He was really struggling to hold her back, because she seemed absolutely willing to get mauled by Benny for a chance to get at Louis. He stood between the two subgroups, a barrier of steely grey fur.

Jayne shrieked. "Esme, stop! It's not Scotty's fault this thing got him—"

There was a bang at the front door. Benny jerked his head in that direction and then back to stare down Rick and Esme. He let out a short, sharp bark.

Phil, we need to end this because they're back.

Jayne looked at Esme. "Honey, I don't know you, but we gotta stick together, okay?"

Esme only glared harder.

Rick raised his hands. "It's okay. I'm...I'm sorry, Phil, we just had a moment... We're all under a lot of stress and..."

"Don't be such a fucking pussy, *Rick*." Esme got up and walked to another room down the hall and slammed the door.

Rick looked like he wanted to cry, but he knew it would just make things worse. Every bit of anger that Phil had at the man for that punch was gone. He knew exactly how deep his wife's words could cut.

Phil tried to nod reassuringly. "It's okay, man, this stress would make anyone...this stress has made us all jumpy."

Rick looked up at him. "Yeah, it's all good. I'm sorry."

Phil stood up and extended a hand to him. "Let's go see what our new friends have to say."

He looked over to Jayne. "Can you watch him?"

Jayne looked back with imploring eyes. "Please... She was wearing a pink summer dress."

Phil leaned down and looked at his son, but talked to the man inside of him. "We're going out there now. Do you need to tell me anything?"

Louis looked down at the bonds holding him and back up. "We run out of time whilst you dither. If you value the life of your son, you will need to act."

Phil wished he could release the bonds, if only to give his son trapped inside some measure of comfort. "Is Scotty...okay?"

Louis nodded but still appraised Phil coldly. "For now, yes. Tell your woman to lock the door. The Indian woman is merely doors down."

Phil glanced over to Rick, who looked down, shamed again.

Jayne interjected, "I'll lock the door. Be careful out there. Look for her."

Tears filled her eyes as she closed the door behind them and Phil heard the lock click into place.

CHAPTER ELEVEN

PENNY AND DENNY STOOD ALONE on the lawn, but it wasn't Penny or Denny; it was Elizabeth Cromwell and whoever possessed Denny's body. They looked terrible. They were covered in dirt, and big dried piss stains marked the fronts of their shorts. Their eyes were sunken and bloodshot from the drying air, skin blotched and chapping.

The first thing that Phil noticed when he opened the door was that the air was even worse. Dry, bone dry, and full of fine dust lifted into the air by oppressive heat and static electricity.

As if on cue, a dull boom and crackle of dry lightning.

Elizabeth stated flatly, "You must bring Louis Villefort."

The one inside Denny stated, "Many things have come to pass that were unforeseen."

Rick coughed and spat. It hit the concrete and evaporated in seconds. A look passed between them. Things were getting worse. It was hotter and it was dryer.

And then they saw it. Across the street and several houses down, one of the homes looked like a bomb had gone off inside. The car in front of it was crushed, and half of it lay in a neighbor's yard, like it had simply been torn in half.

A child lay amidst the debris, her tiny body intact, but even from this distance the ruin of her form could be seen. She'd torn off her own face and ripped away her own throat.

Rick's hand covered his mouth and his eyes bulged in horror as he wept. "*Ay dios mio, ay dios mio…*"

The children turned in unison to the scene.

Denny squinted and rubbed a filthy hand over a filthy face. "Her name was Penelope Cartwright, originally of Canterbury. She drowned her child in a washbasin after hearing the voice of God. In Bedlam, she seemed so very unlike that, but who can tell?"

Penny shrugged. "Yet Villefort found her worthy. A pity."

Rick continued his mantra, tears falling from his face to evaporate on the baking concrete.

The kids turned back to them and their expressions hardened.

"Bring Villefort out here. We must away from this island..." She looked around, her face a mix of anger, wonder, and horror. "This accursed place."

Benny sneezed and coughed, and no one said anything for a few moments.

Phil asked, "Where is Wendy Simmons? Bring her here and we'll consider letting you *talk* to...Louis Villefort."

Denny and Penny turned to one another but didn't speak. They turned back.

"Abigail Bertrand. A sodomite and laudanum drinker. In Bedlam, she earned her keep on all fours. But in the end her guards ended up in the soup."

Rick stopped crying, wiping the back of his hand across his face. "How many people...how many people did it get last night?"

Penny and Denny turned and conferred briefly, wordlessly again, then turned back.

Denny said, "Many."

Penny nodded. "This...thing was not known to us; the Space Between the Spaces is largely unknown. Villefort never mentioned this thing to us."

There was a pause, and Phil took up where he left off. "If you want to speak with Villefort, bring her to us."

Penny, or Elizabeth Cromwell, laughed. "We will not trade one of ours just to speak with Villefort."

Phil laughed back, doing better at sounding confident. "Then have a fantastic night."

He turned and grabbed Rick by the elbow, pulling him back toward the front door, signaling that this meeting was over.

"Hold!" Denny spoke, a desperation cutting through his voice.

Phil looked over his shoulder at Denny and Penny having one of their wordless consultations. They turned from one another to him. Denny asked, "When?"

CHAPTER TWELVE

PHIL AND RICK WATCHED PENNY and Denny cross the street and fade away between the houses. In an hour, they were going to be given Jayne's daughter in exchange for Penny being allowed to speak with Louis Villefort. This would be an interesting conversation to observe.

But Phil didn't like it. He'd come to terms with the impossible scenario. They were stuck in a part of the subdivision surrounded by a bank of clouds that those things lived in, and all the kids under the age of ten seemed to have become hosts to other personalities that claimed they were from Bedlam in the late 1800s.

They were homicidal at best.

But one of those kids was Scotty, and he seemed to be hosting their leader.

And now, they'd be facilitating a conversation between the leader and his troops in exchange for Jayne's daughter, Wendy, currently occupied by one Abigail Bertrand, described as a sodomite and laudanum drinker. From Bedlam.

Phil turned to go back inside but Rick tapped him on the shoulder, stirring him from his fugue. "Hang on a second, we need to talk. You don't like this, do you?"

"Nope, not one bit. But we get Jayne's kid." Phil coughed, the air drying out his windpipe with every breath.

"Do you think they're gonna try to pull something? This Abigail Bertrand might be their Trojan horse."

Phil shrugged; good options were clearly out of the question. "Something, yeah. We're gonna need to watch that kid like a fucking hawk."

Rick nodded. "Yeah, but I think we'll lose Jayne without. Eventually she'll run off on her own and look for her kid."

Phil shook his head and managed a really bitter smile. "Well, at least you don't have kids to worry about here."

Rick let out a sad little laugh. "Yeah, our nieces are enough for me, thank God they weren't here when this shit went down. Esme would have gone crazy for real."

Phil didn't say anything, but he wasn't really good at hiding his expression under the current circumstances. *Esme ain't crazy for real right now?*

Rick exhaled hard. "Yeah, she's…got a temper." He paused for a few moments, then continued. "We can't have kids and she wanted to so bad. The whole thing has really fucked her up. We're in the process of trying to adopt, but that takes time. I think babysitting the girls is all that keeps her sane."

A hard, cold chill crept down Phil's spine despite the heat. "The girls?"

Rick smiled for the first time. "Yeah, her sister drops them off almost every morning. We moved here just so Esme could be near them. Fucking thank God they went to Port Arthur, Felix's got a big boat down there."

Phil's spine was now ice. "Felix?"

Rick nodded. "Yeah, Felix Rosales, your neighbor. Rhonda is Esme's sister."

The dry air turned hard on Phil's throat and he coughed, doubling over from the impact. It hurt, he felt a hint of rusty blood taste, but he was grateful that it rendered his expression unreadable.

Benny killed Esme's niece. Phil had no illusions of what that detail would do to their merry little gang. The second she found out she'd start trying to kill Benny, and Benny was the principal reason those kids hadn't launched any more attacks. He protected them, and he prevented them from having to hurt, or kill, little kids to defend themselves. Given that they were not merely sadistic murderers, but fucking cannibals to boot, made the idea of fighting them terrifying. They wouldn't win. They'd be killed horribly, and then they'd be eaten.

Phil scrunched his eyes shut because tears were burning them. Yeah, he was a beta male whose best friend was a dog, but from where he stood, he didn't want it any other way. Casey had been his best friend, and he married her for it and thought that things would never change. But they did, and now his best friend was his dog. And he'd be fucking god damned if anyone was going to kill his best friend. All he needed was Scotty and Benny, that's it. If he went through life and others viewed him as a broken man, a failed man, the walking wounded from life's calamities, then so be it, but he wasn't going to lose Benny, or Scotty for that matter.

"Look, man, I know how you feel… She's unstable." Rick

interrupted his stream of revelations and resolutions.

"How on earth could you know how I feel?" Phil spoke before his brain kicked into gear.

Rick had his hand on Phil's shoulder, but stepped back and held his hands in the air. "Okay, man, I don't know how you feel. I don't know you from Adam, but I know you gotta defend yours and Esme stepped over the line. Just...hear me."

Phil looked up, teary, to see Rick fighting tears of his own. "I love her. She's all I ever wanted, and after all the bad shit that's happened, I gotta take care of her."

Phil held his breath for a moment. He didn't want to hear Rick's tale of woe, he didn't want to get any closer to Rick and Esme than he was now, and he couldn't ever imagine a situation where he'd hear what was sure to follow—any situation other than the impossibility that they were now immersed in.

He put his hand on Rick's shoulder and lied through his teeth. "It's okay, man, you can talk to me."

Rick squeezed his eyes shut and leaned against the wall of the porch. "I went to Iraq and I got all fucked up, I came back and I was in the VA in El Paso for a while. I was out of it, man, bad. She didn't know what to do. She'd fallen in with some...people while I was away, she was partying too much..."

He stopped and buried his face in his hands. Phil watched tears fall through his fingers to the ground, practically evaporating before they came to rest.

"She got drunk at a party and passed out. She didn't even know who it was did it to her and she had an abortion. But you gotta know, that's not who we are, that's not who she is, that ain't what she's about. It's a sin, and now she can't have kids and all this..."—he pointed to the world around them, the little world that encapsulated this part of Blackwood Estates—"...all this? This is hell, or might as well be in Esme's head."

***

Jayne buried her face in Phil's shoulder and cried till he felt wetness down the front of his shirt. He couldn't help but think that he would have given years off of his life to have Jayne Simmons (AKA White Escalade Blonde From Over by the Trails) giving him the time of day, much less being so grateful to him that she cried. But life works in mysterious ways, and the events of the last day had eclipsed even the basic human need for love and companionship.

He looked down at Louis and Benny looking back at him. Louis had his poker face on, and Benny had his guard dog face on.

He gently pushed Jayne away, and looked around at the array of faces around Jayne's palatial bedroom. He squatted down in front of Louis and rubbed his head the way Scotty always liked. For a brief moment, there was an odd flash of Scotty's smile that mingled with Louis' omnipresent sneer of contempt.

"Okay, Louis, who is Elizabeth Cromwell and what does she want?"

"A one-eyed whore in a kingdom of the blind." He added, "My queen," with a laugh.

Phil knelt down to look at him at eye level. "We are exchanging Jayne's daughter, Wendy, for an opportunity for this Elizabeth Cromwell to talk to you. You're their leader. What does she want?"

"She wants to live free of men that would remove a little girl's eye to pay her father's gambling debts. One-eyed little girls make for inexpensive whores."

Jayne gasped, a tremor passing through her voice. "That's…sick…" Her voice trailed off and a look of disgusted revelation crossed her face. Even this late in the game her mind was fighting acceptance of their situation, the truth of the impossibilities they were facing.

Esme whispered without looking up, "This isn't happening, this isn't happening…"

CHAPTER THIRTEEN

LLOYD H. REYNOLDS, ESQUIRE, HAD seen many shocking things in his life, many disturbing things, and God knows he relished most of them. But many years ago, he had seen the Sublimity that lay beneath the thin veil of the mundane.

Now, when the shocking raised its head, he knew that time was of the essence. He must discover, he must know whether the visitation of the shocking was a sign. Others, he knew, had the gift and could tell outright whether their experience was in fact a sign. But alas, he was not born with that gift. In fact, he wasn't born with much at all, but Lloyd H. Reynolds, Esquire, was no dummy.

"A man's got to do what a man's got to do" was one of his useless father's most grating clichés, mainly because Lloyd's father never did a single thing, at least not to the extent that would have made it worth doing. He'd worked the shrimp boats in Galveston Bay, a little here, a little there. Sometimes swung a machete cutting sugar cane. But while the holes in his shoes never were on the mend, the holes in his pockets were the biggest holes of all.

Lloyd hated him. Hated his uselessness, his laxity and laziness. His bovine stupidity. Lloyd vowed from an early age that he would be nothing like him.

Lloyd would do exactly what a man had to do, and he'd get paid for doing it.

Lloyd took it in the ass. He sucked a lot of dick and he took it in the ass.

It wasn't until the mid-70s that Lloyd heard the word "gay." He'd always heard of those people who did what he did called queers, faggots, and rough trade.

He liked the term "gay." It put a name to a face, a word to a deed, but that didn't last, at least not for Lloyd H. Reynolds, Esq. He'd fucked a million men and would fuck a million more before the truth of it came to him.

He didn't like men, or boys, or little boys.

He liked their *bodies*.

He liked the way they writhed in ecstasy or agony, he liked that place where there was no distinction between the two.

It was at the home of a rich man in River Oaks in Houston, at a party for the rich men of River Oaks in Houston, that he'd touched it. The Sublimity. He'd been tied, whipped, bloodied. Humiliated and degraded.

He'd seen it in that man's eyes, in all of those men's eyes as they systematically reduced him to nothingness. He should have been horrified, he should have been terrified, repulsed, disgusted. But he wasn't. He came, and he came again.

He was thrown out of a car like piece of trash, left for dead on the side of the highway, but Lloyd H. Reynolds did not die. He lived, and he planned, and for the first time in his life, he *knew*.

The important thing to understand about knowing, *true* knowing, is that it becomes an end in and of itself, a religion, a path, a quest, an addiction that nothing can allay. He healed, and he visited that rich man in River Oaks in Houston, and that rich man paid him handsomely to never return or speak his name again.

Lloyd opened a bar in Montrose. Up front it was just another gay leather bar, but beneath the veneer it became a temple for those like himself. Those who knew that the body was a vehicle for experiencing the Sublimity, and that no rules, no laws, no excuses of morality or conscience would suffice. It became both church and laboratory.

And the experiments became rituals, and the rituals became dangerous.

Lloyd had become just as that rich man from River Oaks in Houston.

He got arrogant, and he got sloppy.

One of their rituals became something else entirely.

They'd procured a boy on the streets and paid him in crystal. Then they'd wrapped him in saran wrap and electrocuted him anally. All the assembled celebrants gasped and panted, near the edge as that boy convulsed, involuntarily aroused.

As he came, they all came.

What they hadn't planned on was the part where he died. His heart gave out from methamphetamine and electrocution.

They put him in a chemical barrel in the back storeroom of Lloyd's bar to dissolve in concentrated acid. A simple process, but the best laid plans of mice and men…

The air conditioner failed, and the soup of human and acid in that barrel heated up and a wave of putridity and acrid tang wafted out over the neighboring apartments. Very soon the police arrived and followed their noses.

Lloyd was arrested for murder and was placed on trial.

What he discovered was that the law could bend and take any shape that could be desired, provided that enough lawyerly acumen and money could be brought to bear.

He got off, now a hero for speaking truth to power about the bigotry facing gay men and women everywhere, and especially in Houston. And he was right about those things, but what others never understood about Lloyd H. Reynolds, Esquire, was that he wasn't really gay.

He was something else entirely.

He went to college and then law school, and made ungodly amounts of money defending those who needed to be defended, all in the service of making *who* he was—*what* he was—too dangerous to investigate.

Sure, there were some close calls. An Out-Youth facility he haunted got investigated, and his name was mentioned, but the DA learned to look the other way, just in time to get re-elected.

Yes, life had in fact worked out for the son of an itinerant menial laborer, but as in all things, the pleasures faded and the Sublimity slipped between the fingers of his outstretched grasping hand. The merely physical, no matter how perverse or extreme, became a place of diminishing returns. He had to put it aside, to deny that aspect if he wished to continue his ascent of the winding step.

The pain was exquisite.

He brought in intravenous blood to prevent his death, he stayed awake for three days and three nights, and when he was through he had no external genitalia.

He ate the remnants. His stimulation would need to come from elsewhere.

He began to explore, to meditate, to call out to the universe. He discovered that his will must be shaped further. For days he'd hung suspended from a cross of hooks he built himself; for days he lay on a bed of nails; for days he burned his flesh, and only in that moment did he know what he must do to return to the Sublimity.

He constructed the box and filled it with spiders. He placed himself and a young boy inside and closed the lid. The pain they shared brought the visions, and the visions brought communion with the Sublimity. It called to him, and spoke of paths between the worlds, of time without limit, of oceans of dreams and seas of ash. Of places where the dead go to be born anew, of the past, of the future, of other lives, and of the Space

Between the Spaces. He emerged from the box a new man, but that boy did not emerge at all.

He had vanished.

And this, he found, was the toll to be paid to Charon.

The box was no mere place of horror, no torture device. It was a vehicle to climb the winding stair, and the world would never run out of missing boys to fuel it. Every time he entered, every time he placed a drugged boy-child alongside him, fully aware of the terror that awaited that boy, he became as tempered metal, cleansed of the impurities of this world and wise beyond standard mind.

He learned to harvest their screams, to make essences of their nightmares, to cultivate them all, each a flower, a thing of beauty. And thus his garden grew, power and wisdom to ward off the minor spirits of the abyss.

But last night, something went terribly awry. He'd followed the course of the stars, as he learned, and the timing would be most providential. He entered with a boy named Timmy, procured through the usual means. The spiders envenomed them, and his mind became attuned due to their unique neurotoxin. This had been an arduous tolerance to acquire, but it was required to see further into the belly of the abyss, into the lungs of the Sublimity.

But last night, something went terribly awry. He visited a place he'd never seen, a place he could not imagine, a place he'd only read about in the fragments of a manuscript called *The Song of the Death God*. It was a featureless stone plain, almost perfectly smooth. Red stone and sandy grit the only things to be seen, apart from an almost invisible blue mist.

He found himself with his ear to the ground, listening to a deep thrumming in the earth, a pulse that formed into words of a dead language, a cavernous chant.

And then he looked up.

The sky was a solid curtain of boiling, ink-black clouds, churned and whipped by unseen winds.

And then it happened. A scream, a roar, a blasting trumpet to shatter bones like glass and liquefy flesh. The tumultuous clouds began to congeal, to form a solidity from the gaseous state, to coagulate into coherent form, the wretched, nauseous form of catastrophic tentacles, miles in length.

They descended upon him in the blink of an eye and enveloped him in their fecal embrace, squeezing, crushing, killing…

And he awoke. Not *in* the box. *Outside* the box.

He opened the lid. The boy was still there, shrieking and convulsing.

He would have to be dealt with, but not now.

Lloyd yanked him from the inside, and roughly hung him on the X-shaped cross that shared the room with the box, strapping a ball gag on his face.

This was not supposed to happen. He'd never traveled to that place before, and hadn't intended to go there. What had gone wrong?

He didn't know, but it was somehow already morning. Time to head out front and water the flowers, his wards against the minor denizens of the abyss.

While he had failed last night, and did not know why, his flowers would not fail him if something unintended came through from the Space Between the Spaces.

He would deal with the boy later, after tending to the flowers and meditating in his own special way.

CHAPTER FOURTEEN

IT WAS HOT, TERRIBLY HOT. Texas in August is a hot place, but this place that was, but was not, Texas was much worse. It was blisteringly hot and bone dry. To breathe through the nose hurt, to breathe too quickly through the nose would quickly induce a nosebleed. To breathe through the mouth was worse.

A dry tongue in a dry mouth is a wretched smelling thing. The teeth feel as if they have separated ever so slightly, just enough to feel the dry air pass between them. Upon each exhale, the smell grows worse.

They'd been very careful. Jayne Simmons of course had bottled water, and they'd drained the rear of each toilet in the house as a backup. Other houses had toilets too, and surely someone had to have a swimming pool.

They passed around the second bottle of moisturizing lotion, something expensive smelling with a French sounding name, and even in this moment Phil smiled inwardly, imagining what he'd have given not even a day past to be rubbing lotion on Jayne Simmons's neck.

But now she smelled like a barn animal, and he knew that he smelled even worse. Earlier they'd cleared out the fridge, tossing everything that had spoiled out into her immaculate back yard. He could smell that too.

A dry ripeness.

Yes. His author's sense of aesthetics liked that one, even if his nose disagreed. She turned around and took the bottle from him, squeezed out a dab into her perfectly manicured and immaculately soft hands, and began to rub it across his face.

He closed his eyes and her fingers spread the lotion over his eyelids. For a moment, her fingers were heaven.

He opened his eyes. Maybe she smiled, probably not. Her beautiful face was now marred by a deep jagged scrape across her right cheek, yesterday's makeup a blur across her features.

She whispered like a lost thing. "You're going to get her back and…and…"

He nodded quickly, careful to exhale slowly. "Yeah, it's gonna work out. I'm sure of it, pretty sure…"

She looked down and a tear formed in the corner of her eye and she squeezed them shut. It burned.

Then they heard it: screaming, a whistle emerging from the throats of many, many children. "They're here."

***

They heard her far before they saw her. Wendy Simmons's guest, Abigail Bertrand, was making it clear that her handover in exchange for Elizabeth Cromwell's opportunity to discuss matters with Louis Villefort was a betrayal of the gravest sort. She really didn't like being sold out like this. They had her tied to the wheelbarrow just like the hapless maid from earlier. She was gagged, but still the spittle flew, and charges of treason rained from her lips.

Phil, Rick, and Benny faced off against the crowd just as before, this time joined by Scotty. But right now, it was Louis Villefort, not Scotty, that was steering the ship. They had all agreed that Elizabeth Cromwell would use Jayne's motherhood emotions to leverage the exchange, so she and Esme stayed inside.

There were far fewer kids arrayed in front of them than last time. Last time there could have been fifty; now there appeared to be about thirty. They looked much worse now. They were filthy, hair dry and matted, clothes piss-stained and shit-smeared. Their skin looked like it was sunburned and peeling, but it wasn't the sun that did this. It was the air itself.

And the children had been busy. There were light poles up and down these streets, and from each hung a grisly display of dead cats and dogs.

Louis, speaking through Scotty, asked the question: "How many were taken?"

Elizabeth Cromwell, speaking through Penny, responded: "Twenty-seven by the last count. It is possible that some are still hiding, or are trapped, but it is unlikely."

Louis nodded. "Agreed, this is unlikely."

Rick shook his head and snarled. "Say what you gotta say, and make it fucking fast or we're taking that kid."

Penny and Denny looked at one another and looked back to them.

Then their eyes fell back to Louis. Penny Spoke: "Conditions grow worse. We must away, and very soon. The Hunters of the Outer Dark will come again once the light fails."

Louis nodded. "What information do you possess that I do not?"

Penny shook her head. "None." She paused, then proceeded. "How did this thing happen?"

Louis' lips turned into an angry sneer. "You doubt me. This is unfortunate. Perhaps I overestimated your abilities, your resolve."

Elizabeth Cromwell shook her head rapidly, a panic crossing her features. "No! By no means!"

Louis cocked his head. "But still, you wish to know." He looked from face to face amongst the crowd of children. "You all wish to understand why we are here, why we are not on the other side of the Thames as was intentioned."

None of the children responded, but all were rapt.

He spoke as if explaining the simplest of things to those who could not understand the simplest of things. *"Lorsque les étoiles s'alignent, nous ouvrirons une porte sur l'espace entre les espaces."*

The assembled children just looked at him in even greater confusion and fear, but it wasn't just them who had no idea.

Rick growled. "In English, you little asshole."

Louis shook his head in disgust. "Monsieur Darwin would dismay at the degeneracy required for you to exist."

Rick was about to react when Phil put a hand on his arm and shook his head. "Don't engage him. That's what he wants."

Phil nodded and gave Louis a little shake, but not too much as he was bound with several belts. "Okay, Louis, you've got everyone's undivided attention. Quite an audience. Now, do you know why this"— he motioned all around—"all of this, is happening, or not? I'm betting that you don't have a clue."

Louis smirked and spoke slowly: "Time is different there."

Rick snapped, "Where? Where is time different?"

Louis looked to Rick. "You saw what happened at the border. Time accelerated, did it not? We were there for mere moments, but time passed as if we had been there for hours. In the Space Between the Spaces, *in spatia inter,* time and distance mean nothing. Minutes and eternities are the same."

It took a moment, but Rick responded. "That's interesting, but it doesn't explain why you are here."

Louis nodded. "I have considered, and concluded. Another has performed rites of a similar nature, causing our course across the heavens to be detoured to this accursed place."

Denny, or the one in Denny, blurted out, "But what do we do, my lord?"

Louis, for the first time, looked uncertain. Phil wasn't sure anyone else saw this, but he knew Scotty's face, every motion, every gesture, every single expression that could cross it.

Louis cleared his throat. "There is a sort of balance, a kind of synchronicity, a pattern to the falling of leaves and the breath of this world. It is not as simple as the rotation of gears and levers, *but it is there* for those with eyes to see. The Other One. The one who performed these rites that brought us here…" He paused. "He is here. Somewhere in here, with us."

CHAPTER FIFTEEN

LLOYD H. REYNOLDS, ESQUIRE, WAS no coward. He had seen things and done things that would leave a strong man an emotional cripple for the rest of his godforsaken life. But Lloyd H. Reynolds was not an emotional cripple, or a cripple of any sort for that matter. He was strong, and his life would be no godforsaken thing, because Lloyd H. Reynolds, Esquire, was his own god.

And to a man like Lloyd, that is what it was all about. *I will ascend into heaven, I will exalt my throne above the stars of God: I will sit also upon the mount of the congregation, in the sides of the north. I will ascend above the heights of the clouds; I will be like the most High.*

Lloyd didn't know much about the Bible and believed even less of it than he knew, but that one line had always stuck with him from the day his daddy had decided getting saved was his ticket out of being a piece of shit.

It hadn't worked, and Daddy was drinking and jerking off by the end of the day. Lloyd heard him crying about it, but no amount of guilt kept him from jerking off while he did it.

Yes, this world was a veil of tears, but only for those too weak to do anything about it. Yes, this life was a shitstorm, but he was the one supposed to be doing the shitting—it was for others to eat, not him. He'd done his time on all fours and had calluses on his hands and knees to prove it.

Someone or something was fucking with him, because there was no way his experiments with the universe could have caused this…whatever it was.

The Morales girls and two others he recognized from one street over killed Edwina. They didn't just kill her, they disemboweled her.

He'd watched. Like little hunters they'd stalked her, and she'd known instinctively what these little creatures intended. But she was fat and old and unused to being hunted by things more hyena than child.

They'd caught her, bound her feet with string, torn out her eyes, and cut her open. Practiced, efficient, and ritual. They spoke words he didn't recognize but didn't have to know in order to divine their meaning. This cat, and those creatures like her, could not, would not, be tolerated because *they knew*.

Cats, and those like them, knew instinctively what these children were, or more likely, what rode them.

Had these things, whatever they were, escaped from the Sublimity? He'd thought about it all morning after seeing them retreat.

But it wasn't him that they'd retreated from. And it certainly wasn't from that moron Phil, who happened to wander over at that point. *It was from his dog.*

Granted, Benny was a seriously dangerous dog, but still…

And the words that little girl had said before running off. "You appear as a servant of Ithaqua, yet you cozen these Sons of Adam. You must be…"

That part was a real head scratcher. Ithaqua was some kind of Native American god or devil or some such, but Lloyd knew nothing of creatures like that, creatures from what he'd come to think of as deeper *layers* of the Sublimity.

He knew other men had traveled the paths he had traveled, and he knew that each one had done so by his own means unless they had been taught by another, or had learned what another knew by reading his writings, but Lloyd only knew of such writings peripherally.

Should he attempt another trip to the Sublimity to try to trace what had happened? He shook his head. Too risky. Not after what he'd observed happening shortly after the incident with the little girls and Edwina.

It wasn't just those five little girls. As far as he could tell, it was every single little kid in this subdivision. And it was only this subdivision, or at least part of it as far as he could tell. There was no cellphone signal, there was no electricity. And a spontaneous rampage by all the little kids should have brought the cops, but there were no cops.

He'd watched as that fat Mexican dipshit got stabbed by one of those little girls, right through the hand. Blondie in the yoga pants had pulled up and saved him and his little *chica* from becoming bean dip. They'd left their absurd little Prius, doors open, right in the middle of the street. It was still running, last he'd checked.

He watched as they'd come to the corner of Maypole and met up with Phil, then it looked like they'd all went down Maypole, presumably to Jayne Simmons's house.

No cops, combined with the fact that they'd gone down Maypole instead of out the other way to get out of the subdivision, told him that there was no getting out of the subdivision.

From the second story of his house he saw all these things, and he saw the clouds, and he did the math. He wasn't going to be driving out of here. No, he would have to employ alternate means to get the job done.

Lloyd H. Reynolds, Esquire, smiled in the dark, but the dark was a different place when the air was like this. He could feel the skin stretch across his face, and it felt wrong. All wrong, like chapped lips in a cold wind or sunburned skin rubbing against stiff, rough fabric.

And in that moment, he knew that this problem was going to get exponentially worse, and it was going to kill him if he didn't thread this needle in a timely fashion. He didn't know what it was that had rampaged through Blackwood Estates last night, but he'd heard the crashing and splintering of several houses and the unreal shrieks of children caught by these rumbling nightmare things. He wasn't stupid enough to look at them, he knew better than that. He also knew that one of them had walked down the middle of his street, but when it passed his house it had detoured through the neighbors' yards across from him. These things didn't care for his special flowers one bit.

He also knew his flowers would be dead very soon without water, and then those things would come to find out what manner of creature could ward them away like that.

But his smile returned, followed by a bitter little chuckle of irony. His system of magic, unlike other systems, was not dependent upon any kind of calendar, astrological or not. He would be away from this place before they could come for him.

Lloyd felt around the space in front of him until his hands fell across the switch. Deep red lights broke through the blackness and a whir of little fans kicked in, both to help provide just the right temperature and humidity for the hundreds of baby mice and the enormous black widow spiders that he fed them to.

He had a bank of truck batteries to make sure that power never failed to his house. If he was travelling in the Sublimity, narcotized by the venom of these spiders, and the alarms did not wake him, he could be lost forever.

He put on his gloves and carefully, very carefully, removed five of his most reliable ladies. He walked into his ritual chamber, also completely sealed off from the sun, and turned on the light, waking his guest.

He would need to send the boy ahead of him to make sure the way was clear.

CHAPTER SIXTEEN

ABIGAIL BERTRAND, THE ONE INSIDE Jayne's daughter, though bound viciously, had managed to chew through the gag covering her mouth. "I know who it is, my lord! I know the very one!"

Elizabeth Cromwell, the one inside Penny, smashed her squarely in the face, the punch making a nasty popping sound as it connected with her jaw. Her head jerked in the opposite direction and her eyes fluttered as she fell out of consciousness.

Rick jumped, and Benny jumped, and Phil almost followed. Luckily he had one hand on Scotty's/Louis' shoulder and the other hand full of leash. "Rick, no!"

Benny immediately sat, and Rick stopped dead in his tracks as a shield wall of garden tools and sharpened pool cues snapped into place, forming a lethal picket that would have spelled his end had he taken but a few steps more.

Elizabeth Cromwell smiled.

Louis shook his head and sighed, then laughed a mirthless laugh. "Your stratagem has been foiled, my dear Elizabeth."

She shrugged and a cold ruthlessness filled her eyes. "You taught me to never walk into a room that I cannot escape, but don't worry, my lord, there are designs within designs."

Rick edged back to his side of the standoff. "The fuck does that mean, you little bitch?"

Elizabeth Cromwell's smile became broader and colder. "It means this."

She pulled out a knife and held open Abigail Bertrand's left eye, holding the tip of the blade to her exposed eyeball. Blood poured from her mouth from the wicked punch, and she stared up the shaft of the blade pointing into her left eye.

Phil's vision constricted and his breath held fast; he knew that this game was probably lost.

Elizabeth Cromwell stared right into Phil's eyes. "You will give us Louis Villefort now, or we will take this dear, dear child as our supper. I believe the mother of the one she inhabits will wish to watch this feast, do you not?"

Too fast, too fast, too fast. Phil's mind raced for an out as he heard frantic feet pounding down the stairs behind him and Jayne flinging open the door and rushing out onto the porch, shouldering past him and running heedless into the phalanx...

He grabbed her shoulders and pinned her, squirming and screaming, on the dry brittle grass. She screamed what all mothers do. "My baby, my baby. Please, God, don't hurt my baby!"

Elizabeth Cromwell opened her mouth and let a stream of black spit fall from the tip of her tongue onto Abigail Bertrand's forehead.

Jayne's screams stopped abruptly as they watched the foul spittle congeal into a spider thing that sprouted legs from every axis and rolled off her forehead and onto the grass below, then jettisoned away as a sphere made of terrible hairy little legs. In the grasping silence they swore they heard an angry squealing as it pinwheeled away.

Louis, inside Scotty, broke the stunned silence. "Elizabeth. We had a compact with these people. Give them Abigail."

Elizabeth, who had been gloating down into Abigail's petrified eyes, swung her head back to him, eyes burning with fury. "You cannot mean to give this trollop to these..."

He interrupted her sternly. "You question much, do you not, Elizabeth?"

Her expression went from fury to panic.

In this moment, Phil knew there was more happening here than met the eye.

For tense seconds, Louis stared Elizabeth down with a commanding gaze. "Basic courtesy dictates that you engage honestly with our hosts. We are guests here and you will comport yourself accordingly."

She opened her mouth and cleared her throat. "My lord, *Louis*, I meant no offence. I was merely..."

"No. No more. Bring Abigail here, right now."

Elizabeth looked around the assembly of children's faces looking back at her. Though the cruelty and malevolence still reigned behind their eyes, there was some other thing happening here, some group dynamic at play.

Elizabeth motioned with her head and two of the boys stepped up to steer the wheelbarrow, and Abigail, toward Phil's group.

"No. Stop." Louis sounded like he was getting angry. "Elizabeth, *you* will bring Abigail."

The silence, already deafening, became a cacophony. Elizabeth Cromwell's expression went to icy hatred. She stalked over, shouldering aside the two boys, and began the grunting and pushing of the wheelbarrow across the few meters that separated the two groups.

It wasn't easy. Elizabeth, through Penny, was a little girl, and this was a full-sized wheelbarrow with someone tied to it. This kind of exertion in this terrible dry heat was an agony, and it was obvious now that this was intentional, a punishment and an act of dominance on Louis' part.

CHAPTER SEVENTEEN

LLOYD H. REYNOLDS CRACKED THE front door, then slipped through and crouched behind the enormous flowery bushes that obscured his home's entryway from the view of the street. He shimmied along the side of the house to switch his water from the city supply to his rainwater collection cistern. This vessel, along with the garish garden encircling his house, had been the focus of a hard-fought lawsuit against the Homeowner's Association of Blackwood Estates. They acted like he was just being an uppity queen. He let them run wild with that assumption, and later on used it against them. And he won. They thought it was all about vanity and pomposity. They were wrong.

It was about survival.

And that wasn't all they were wrong about; in fact, a great many people were wrong in a great many regards when it came to Lloyd H. Reynolds, Esquire.

For example, the silly horticulturist who Lloyd caught excitedly gaping at the otherworldly blooms surrounding Lloyd's home.

"Oh my god, I've never seen flowers like these! For the life of me, I can't identify any of these beautiful flowers! Where on earth are they from?"

Lloyd got a restraining order, but still the man persisted. It took a few weeks in jail to finally dissuade the man from continuing down this path of enquiry. Lloyd had no intention or desire to answer the man's questions, or to draw any more attention to his flowers. You may look, but not for too long, and only from a distance.

The answer to the man's question of "Where on earth are they from?" would have led to great pains in explaining, for the simple fact that they weren't from Earth. They weren't even from the universe where this Earth resided.

They were from the Sublimity.

He turned the valve and his fears were fulfilled. Nothing but a weak trickle. The water in the cistern had nearly evaporated entirely.

His flowers were already withering and wilting. Whatever water was left, soon it would be their last. And he needed to water them very soon. Zero humidity would kill them off before nightfall, and when night came, the Hunters of the Outer Dark would come as well. He needed time.

He edged along the wall, back to the porch, and crouched down again behind the bushes, looking up and down the silent street. Dead, washed out, color drained, grass brown, and everything covered in a haze of dust.

Except for his yard. That was hard to miss for anyone watching.

He pulled out his binoculars for a closer look.

Nothing; he was alone, as far as he could tell.

He crouched and ran down the walkway to the little white picket fence surrounding his yard. He'd had to fight the Homeowner's Association about this thing too. He couldn't have little kids trampling his precious flowers.

He looked up and down the street.

Cats and dogs hanging from light poles, intestines spilling from opened abdomens, but no little kids.

Most of the houses were intact but a few were torn apart, looking like they'd been bulldozed, dismantled with steam shovels. The Hunters of the Outer Dark had found their prey within.

Phil's house was the interesting exception. He'd seen Phil pull away in his SUV, then watched as the entire army of little kids had streamed inside, ululating in their unearthly way as they stormed the house. He'd heard screams of frustration and concerted pounding, and then later he'd watched them stream out, covered in what could only be sheetrock dust.

What had those kids been after? That was the question Lloyd wanted to answer.

Still crouched down, he unlatched the little picket gate and slipped through, closing it behind him, then sprinted across the street, straight for Phil's wide-open front door.

It was pretty much what he'd expected. Those kids had dismantled the house, methodically tearing out the sheetrock and insulation beneath. They shredded the couches. Everything in the kitchen had been heaped in the middle of the floor.

Halfway up the gaudy and ornate staircase was a little girl laying facedown.

A very dead little girl, her blood a terrible red-brown splash up and down the stairs, the carpet turned to a nasty crust.

He turned her over, and despite her already desiccated form, it was easy to tell who she was: she was one of his immediate neighbors, one that he'd last seen with her sisters and two other little girls disemboweling Edwina the cat.

One of the Rosales girls.

Her throat was gone, torn all the way free.

Phil's dog, Benny, had done this. This much was plainly obvious.

Had the little kids done all of this trying to find Benny? That didn't make much sense either, because he'd seen Benny in the front seat of Phil's SUV when he'd pulled out, and the kids would have been able to see that too. And if that *had* been the case, and Benny *had* been here, Lloyd was pretty sure there would have been a lot more than just one dead little kid here.

He peered out the back door and saw Phil's vulgar little ghetto rat dead on one of the lawn chairs, a huge barbeque skewer protruding from her back. He smiled and laughed, thinking of Phil fucking her. Then he shrugged. Probably more entertaining than that frigid little twit he'd divorced.

Were the kids looking for Phil's son?

Nothing else made sense, but that made little sense either.

What would they want with a retard?

CHAPTER EIGHTEEN

ELIZABETH CROMWELL GLARED WITH EVERY drop of venom that flowed through the black rivers of hell.

Abigail. Abigail Bertrand. Slut. Cunt. Whore. Usurper.

Dead fucking whore, just as soon as they were away from this deformed place.

Maybe sooner. Maybe.

The two that stood before her would be her passport to this victory. She hadn't sucked off three guards every night to get to Louis' cell, just to allow herself to be tossed aside like spoiled meat to the dogs. Lapped up and puked out and lapped up again.

She was not trash. She may have lived out dirty trash games to survive, but inside she knew she was meant for more. She was born for greatness, but she had never known what form that greatness was to take. Not until she had seen his proud face, his black and determined eyes; not until she had looked in those eyes and seen the god inside him.

They'd forced all of them in the wretched tenement schools to learn about Greek gods. They were covered in fleas and lice, and most could not read, but still they were forced to memorize the names of gods worshipped by people dead thousands of years.

And that is exactly what he was. A god. Aloof, haughty, capricious, and wrathful. Wise and far seeing, a traveler who knew the music of the spheres. She was born to serve him; she was born to be his.

The two standing before her waited patiently. Andrea Hendry and Tristina Thorne. Now ensconced in brown skin and brown eyes and black hair.

Pretty, she thought, in an aboriginal way.

Did not people like these live in the jungles of Mexico? What could they possibly be doing in this sterile modernity?

They lived here. Their name was *Rosales*.

Juanita and Monica Rosales. Sisters of Mary Rosales, recently deceased. Recently murdered by the wolf, *German shepherd*, owned by Phil, father of Scotty, in whom her love was imprisoned.

Apparently, some kind of simpleton.

She knew what Penny knew, and Andrea and Tristina knew what Juanita and Monica Rosales knew. And they knew a very important thing. They knew that their Aunt Esme was a very sad woman who doted upon them constantly because, as their mother had explained to them with the utmost sensitivity, she could not have children of her own.

Yes, their poor Aunt Esme...

Poor, poor mad Aunt Esme...

CHAPTER NINETEEN

RICK AND PHIL HAD TIED her with belts and scarves, and Phil had warned Jayne about all the things that she already knew, that her daughter was no longer just her daughter. Rick nearly lost a finger, but he got his hand in between Jayne's neck and Abigail Bertrand's teeth just in time. She opted for taking a big bite out of Jayne's shoulder as a consolation prize for not being able to kill her. Only the fact that her jaw was injured by Elizabeth Cromwell's wicked punch saved Jayne from even further injury.

Now Rick bandaged Phil's finger while Esme bandaged Jayne's shoulder. It was an ugly bite; Abigail had really gone to work, shaking her head like a dog and tearing away flesh. Jayne sobbed in pain, a terrible mother's lament. Her daughter was now someone else.

Phil looked in and wondered if that was the place that every parent found themselves in, for better or for worse, when their child outgrew them and became their own person. Even if their child turned into what every parent would want, there's got to be some sense of loss.

He looked to Benny, who gazed back as if he understood; then he looked over to Scotty, but Louis looked back, and something about his gaze said that he understood too.

In his heart, Phil knew that he would never experience that moment of separation for Scotty, because Scotty would never grow past the level of comprehension that he currently had. There would never be that moment where his son outgrew him and moved on to his own life. There would never be that moment, or so many others, that a father experienced as his boy grew to manhood.

The only thing that would change would be his size, and as he grew, Phil's ability to guide him and care for him and protect him would diminish, until one day Scotty would go to an institution, a glorified prison, a storage facility for those that needed storage. And one day Phil would die, and Scotty would live out the rest of his days in that institution until he too died.

His chest heaved once, and a single tear slid away.

Esme did something that almost looked like a smile. "Fuck, man, it can't hurt that bad."

Phil tried and failed to play it off. "Ahhh, it really does hurt worse than you think."

She fixed him with a judgmental glance and he looked away, only to find himself looking back into Scotty's eyes, but seeing Louis Villefort's mind.

"What is her name, Philip?"

Phil jerked out of his doldrums. "Who? What are you talking about?"

Louis looked down, then looked back and asked quietly, "He doesn't know her name, just that he calls her 'Mommy.'"

Phil didn't say anything.

"What is her name, Phil, and why does she not live with you? She isn't dead, and she used to live with you. What is her name and where is she?"

Phil didn't say anything. The room had gone an ugly kind of quiet.

Jayne spoke. Barely a whisper. "Her name is Casey. She divorced Phil after he got a lot of money publishing his first book."

Rick nodded. "*Rip Crew*. Fucking badass, man."

Part of Phil wanted to blush, but he wasn't at a book signing, smiling and putting his signature on newly purchased copies of his latest. He was here, now.

Phil looked to Jayne. "How did you know that?"

Something like a smile crossed her face. "You were the talk of the town. Everybody wanted to know the famous writer. It was a big deal when you moved into the subdivision."

His brow creased, and his voice went down a few decibels. "How did you know about Casey?"

Jayne shrugged. "Lloyd Reynolds."

Abigail Bertrand sat forward from her place against the wall, her eyes pleading as she shouted something unintelligible from behind her gag.

Louis' expression changed, a look of deep concern crossing his face. "Phil, I ask that you remove her gag, if only for a moment. She seems to have some important information to share." He looked around the room from face to face. "I promise that I will vouchsafe her conduct. From this point forward, without fail, Abigail will obey you, and will harm no one."

Rick scowled and shook his head, and Esme scoffed. "Fuck you."

Phil looked at Jayne, then to Rick and Esme. Then he looked to Louis and Abigail. "You have thirty seconds to say something worth hearing or that gag goes back on."

Then he stepped over and removed the gag, taking great care lest she lunge at his exposed forearms.

He took it off and she gasped. "Mister Reynolds! The sodomite! The flower man! He is the other!"

CHAPTER TWENTY

THAT NIGHT THE HUNTERS OF the Outer Dark came again, their foghorn whale songs splitting the firmament and separating the possessed from the possessors until all that was left were screaming, crying, and dying children. They were torn from their hiding places in closets and underneath beds, and shown things to turn the minds of children toward ending their own lives. With little fingers and scissors, and shards of broken glass, their eyes came before their throats, and the Hunters of the Outer Dark fed, nourished on terror and the uncomprehending confusion of those who were taught that their nightmares were nothing but dreams.

And in those final seconds, the children knew that those nightmares had been the soft spots in reality where their wandering minds had glanced upon the Sublimity and those hungry things that walked the silent corridors of those outer planes. And they knew, too, that this death was just the beginning of their time in the terrible maw of their own hell.

***

Benny lay curled around Scotty. His head was down, but his ears were up. They'd taped black garbage bags over the glass of the window to prevent any light from leaking out.

Jayne clutched a golf club and wept, tears falling down the sides of her face to the carpet beneath her. They stung her dried and burning skin, and stung her seared eyes, but she couldn't stop. Because what she heard out there in this night place were children dying, children whose parents she knew, little girls and boys who rode little bikes up and down the sidewalks of the world that had come before.

Her daughter and Scotty lay next to her, having drunk a half-bottle of cough syrup each, more than enough to keep them dead asleep. It had actually been Louis' idea, so that they couldn't cry out, so that the possessed wouldn't be parted from the possessor by the unearthly songs of these Hunters of the Outer Dark.

***

She cried, too, because she knew the danger that Phil and Rick and Esme faced: that they might not return from their jaunt, this fool's errand to the world outside the house.

This had been Louis' idea too.

They would go and capture the "other," the black magician who had caused this thing to be born into their world.

Lloyd Reynolds.

Louis had laid out a compelling case. Lloyd surely would not leave when the Hunters were about on their hunt. And the children would be in hiding as soon as they heard the songs of the Hunters.

All that Rick and Esme and Phil had to do was not get caught.

CHAPTER TWENTY-ONE

IT TOOK PHIL MERE SECONDS to regret this idea. It was a good idea, the best one they had, and the one most likely to succeed. But they hadn't counted on what would lay beyond the windows and walls they'd hid behind.

It was dry, painfully dry.

They'd smeared a thin layer of Vaseline over every inch of skin not covered by clothes. Phil had tried to clean his skin earlier, before the Vaseline, using one of the crate loads of disposable sanitary wipes in Jayne's bathroom linen closet.

That had been a mistake. There was alcohol in those wipes and it burned like it did every time he'd cleaned a skinned knee. But this wasn't skinned, it was just drier than human skin is supposed to be.

As dry as the vacuum of space.

As dry as the Space Between the Spaces.

Rick had been meticulous, almost military, in his planning. They just hadn't known what would be out here with them, what they would find themselves *inside*...

Their first objective was the gate at the back of Jayne's yard.

They would quietly, ever so quietly, open the back door, crouch down, and run to that gate. There was a wide patio with picnic tables and lawn chairs, then there was a large, elevated flower bed, then an open expanse of grass with Wendy's little playground of swings and monkey bars and a slide.

They hadn't made it as far as the flower bed when they knew that this plan had been woefully uninformed. Their feet travelling over the concrete of the patio had sounded like a drum chorus at a high school football game. They ran, crouching down, and leapt up over the little brick wall enclosing the flower garden, their feet crushing dried flowers that exploded into clouds of dust.

It sounded like firecrackers.

They jumped down as they crossed out of the flower garden and into the grass around Wendy's playground. The grass crackled and burst into painful little shards that clung to their skin, burning and itching.

But the sound that was strangest to their ears, the one that stopped Esme in her tracks next to a silly wooden clubhouse with a bright orange plastic slide emerging from its side, was the sound of her own breathing, the sound of all of their breathing. It was enormous, magnified far beyond what it should be, even in this void of sound.

They stood in their tight, tiny circle before the gate, eyes wide as saucers, no words passing between them.

Yes, I'm hearing all these things too.

We hadn't planned on this.

Do we go back? What do we do?

We can't go back… We're out of time… Louis said so, and we all know it, we can all feel it.

We stick to the plan.

Rick nodded, gesturing toward the black metal handle.

I'm going to open it now, be ready.

Phil and Esme nodded, and Phil thought he could even hear his skin crackling as his head moved up and down.

This is silence, this is what it sounds like.

Rick's eyes, what Phil could see of them, reflected a kind of acknowledgement of this statement of truth. Phil turned to Esme, and a tiny nod of her head told that she knew it too. This silence, this utter lack of sound, is more than just a lack of wind and the susurrus and chirp of insects in the Texas night. This silence is a thing in and of itself, a thing that is heard with all five senses just as surely as the shock of an earthquake.

And there was more out here as well.

Even in the absence of all electric light, even in the absence of stars and moon, they should be able to see the dried and dead flower garden they passed through on the way here.

But it was lost in this darkness that lay upon everything like…

Phil thought hard, his writer's mind grasping for a simile or metaphor, something to express a smothering choking blanket when no true words would suffice.

Esme held up a flashlight. *Should I?*

Phil and Rick shook their heads in an emphatic *no.*

She nodded and glanced to the gate. *Let's get moving.*

Rick nodded back, then held up a finger to call for a pause. Their plan had taken into account the dryness of the air. He took a bottle of water from the pocket of his cargo pants and put it to his lips for a small sip, then he poured a bit on a bandanna and placed it to his nose and inhaled. All of them had experienced nosebleeds from the dryness of the air.

We need to do this at regular intervals or we'll all be bleeding like stuck pigs.

It was really, really loud.

Phil and Esme followed suit, and that was really loud too, but nowhere near as loud as the sound of the big black iron handle of the gate as metal rubbed on metal and clacked into place, followed by a grating screech of hinges as the gate door swung open.

They all cringed, their minds even now unable to correlate all of the stars in this constellation into a coherent shape.

When the gate had finished shrieking enough to let them through, they passed into the little alley, their feet crunching a cacophony in the grass, echoing out into the night.

Blackwood Estates, like many subdivisions, had utility easements running behind the backs of fences, providing a narrow alley between one owner's fence and that of his or her neighbor behind them. This little alley would be their secret highway running parallel to Maypole Street, and would dead end, just like Maypole, into Phil and Lloyd's street.

Then they heard the first foghorn blast of the Hunters of the Outer Dark, a sound they could feel down to their bones. It was far away, and to the south, if this place still had a "south." But they knew that it would be shortly joined by its companion, as was the pattern on the previous nights.

They discovered that they had all frozen in their tracks, Rick mouthing the Hail Mary in Spanish, audible here by the motion of his lips alone. He was in front, followed by Esme. Phil brought up the rear. He whispered as quietly as a man could, "Rick, Rick, you gotta move, man."

Rick glanced over his shoulder, nodding his head in acknowledgement.

They started to move forward, heedless of the sound of their feet on the grass or their breathing, things that should ordinarily be as silent as a mouse in an empty kitchen at night, but not here, not now.

Mere moments later, the titanic whale song shattered the stillness again. The same one as before, but this time much closer.

There was a *thump*, loud, far too loud, as Esme dropped her flashlight, and a tiny mewling came from her chest and throat, then the sound of rapid, terrified breathing.

They discovered that they had stopped again, dead in their tracks. They hadn't even been aware that they weren't moving.

Rick turned back to her and put a reassuring hand on her shoulder.

A terrible remorse, a terrible single sob, and she slapped a hand over her mouth.

Again, too much sound, even though no one would ordinarily hear these gestures.

But this place was different.

Far away, but still too close, they could hear the crump and march of many elephantine feet. Like a caterpillar the length of several city blocks, threading its way through yards and streets, trees bending and groaning in its wake. Then a snap of a glass windshield and a dry crack as one of those trees cracked.

All heading in their direction.

Phil hissed, "Run. Now!"

CHAPTER TWENTY-TWO

T HE SLEEPING EXPLORER, HIS WANDERING mind, should know these winding steps. But nothing here was as it should be. He was lost.

Lloyd H. Reynolds took a deep breath in this real world, knowing that these lucid dreams can mix the real and surreal with no warning at all, and that the dreamer must simply exert control to bring these thoughts into alignment with his will...

But it was not working.

He'd sent the boy ahead of him, envenomed, drugged in his unique way, but he came back.

Scratch that, thought Lloyd.

The boy never left at all. He just lay there, sweating, tossing and turning in his harness inside the box.

It's not working, and you know exactly why.

No, it can't be! This should work in Madrid, Addis Ababa, or Shanghai. We are not bound by where or when, we are not bound by time and space at all, so...

You're not in Kansas anymore, Toto.

In fact, you're not on planet Earth, or in the fucking universe where the Earth exists. You're not here, because here *isn't* here *anymore.*

You're in Oz, and you need a plan B.

He slept, but his mind kept spinning on its axis, a trick he'd mastered years before when glimpses of the Sublimity were the goal, before he'd cobbled together the idea for the box.

The world, the universe, the multiverse, the Sublimity is full of seeming coincidences and events without causes, but the literate mind, the wise mind, the true mind sees through the painting to know the hand of the artist, to learn his technique and to know his mind.

This was no accident. Something or someone caused this.

This was not my doing. My intentions were plain and practiced, and each step known. I left nothing to chance because I don't leave things to chance. I don't have accidents.

So what to do, Lloyd?

He sighed, knowing that the minutes and seconds to fix this thing were escaping from him. Then he opened his eyes, and unbuckled his harness, and pushed opened the lid of the box.

He pulled himself out, then reached back inside the box, unbuckled the boy and pulled him out too.

The boy muttered in his torpor, "A penny, a penny, no more, your lordship…"

Lloyd shook his head. These street kids were always stupid or crazy or both.

The boy was limp in his arms, but Lloyd knew better than to leave these things to chance. He looped the rope around his torso and cinched it up until he hung in front of the X-shaped cross, then strapped him on, bound at wrists and ankles.

Lloyd smiled when he saw three of his best ladies still clinging to the boy in their special way. He gently pulled them away, their fangs seeking purchase on his rubber gloves, and affixed them to himself in just the right way, piercing his skin with their mandibles and injecting him with their sweet narcotic venom.

He sighed in a familiar joy as the rigor tensed his muscles as he climbed back in the box, his special ladies hanging from their very special perches. His will would be enough.

CHAPTER TWENTY-THREE

BLOOD LEAKED FROM THEIR NOSES, but didn't run far. It was simply too dry. The blood just coagulated in place, seemingly after just a few seconds. If they could have seen themselves, they would have sworn that the faces looking back had been in some sort of terrible accident.

Truth be told, they really had been in an accident, just not one that could be explained in a sane manner.

But explanations would have to wait. The Hunter had scented its prey, and a trumpeting to shatter bones announced that its mate had been summoned to join in the chase.

The sound of the pursuing Hunters left no need to hide the sound of their flight down the narrow corridor between rear fences, only the absence of light slowed them down. They'd already fallen twice, ending up in a painful pile as dry skin cracked open and fast-drying blood glued the scratching, itching dirt and grass to their skin.

Even moving at a slower pace, they were exhausted immediately.

Esme stopped jogging and doubled over, wheezing in the bone-dry dusty air, retching and coughing. Rick followed suit, while trying to comfort Esme.

Phil looked over his shoulder and caught for a moment a blackness within the blackness, a collection of stars that did not illuminate, but shone in such a way as to draw in light, pulling out what remnants remained in the bones of this lost place...

He jerked his head forward. He knew what would happen if he saw into the heart of the Hunter. He knew that in knowing it, he would be known, that by seeing he would be seen. All it took was open eyes and a matter of seconds, and then his screams would have joined him to the children it had taken the last two nights.

Rick's head turned in the direction of the Hunter, and Phil slapped him painfully, then pushed him forward, stumbling him into Esme.

Through gritted teeth he hissed, "Fucking move or we die!"

But now their way was blocked. From their front, less than a block away, came the earsplitting call of the second Hunter. Esme and Rick looked up, Rick pulling his gaze away quick, but Esme stood transfixed, and a squealing moan escaped her lips.

Phil reached past Rick and wrapped a hand around Esme's head, covering her eyes and pulling her backward. They all fell into a pile as the first Hunter crushed through the fences forming the corridor, no more than three hundred feet behind them.

This is not where they were supposed to be, but they were cut off. The Hunters knew they were in that narrow corridor, the first behind them and the second blocking the mouth of the alley.

They were panting and wheezing and choking on the terrible dry dusty air. Esme was coming close to hyperventilating, and Rick tried in his bumbling way to comfort her, earning only a hiss and a slap that sounded like a gunshot in the void of sound.

Phil hissed back, gritting, "They're too close, get your shit in order!"

They stopped their absurd struggling, and in the tiny available light, he saw their faces, swollen and burned by the terrible dry air, scratched and cracked, scabbed and gouged.

Phil reached up and to his left, grabbed the handle of the gate, and pushed them all into Sean Leonard's back yard. He was a programmer at some hotshot software company and the subdivision's hookup for weed; Phil had spent a few afternoons out here with Sean, smoking his pain away. A pool lay between them and the back door. Not far, but too far to see in this lightless place.

Phil pulled them up from their pile, and they gathered around the pool. As he got close enough, he could see that their fears were validated. This pool—and it wasn't a small pool, either—was almost completely empty. The dry air had sucked it all away.

They staggered toward the back door and Rick gasped and coughed. "I hope you've got a plan, man, or we're fucking dead."

Phil fished around in a potted plant next to the big glass double doors. "Just keep it together, and don't look at them."

The plant, bush, shrub, whatever it had been, was completely dead, its leaves fallen and desiccated, crumbling into dust when touched. He quested about in the leaves, eventually pulling out the key, and they piled through the back door.

Phil risked a glance backward but saw nothing, except for the amorphous outlines of the two Hunters. He quickly averted his gaze.

Rick grabbed Esme's hand. "That's our cue. We gotta—"

He stopped speaking. Esme had found Sean.

Obviously, he'd been home when everything happened, probably sitting at his desk coding away as his office, right off the kitchen where they stood now, was completely wrecked.

Even though his corpse had been dried and shriveled in this terrible air, his death had been more terrible still. There was a dent in his head above his right temple. He was bound at the ankles with a belt. His arms were not bound, because they'd been cut off and nailed to the wall next to him. A hammer and a hacksaw lay near the corpse.

Sean had a daughter named Melody. She was probably eight, by Phil's reckoning.

She hung inverted from a rope slung over the door, throat slashed, a ring of blood dried in a crock pot positioned beneath her. She'd been bled, and as they looked around at one another, the reasoning became very clear: The kids of Bedlam ate their own, or at least drank their blood in a pinch.

Melody had killed her father and then, some time later, she'd been killed too.

Phil leaned down and fished through Sean's pockets, pulling out his phone. He remembered an important thing about Sean. He was very serious about not being disturbed before two in the afternoon, as that was his prime time. He drank around ten cups of coffee and a half-dozen red bulls and coded whatever it was that made him so much money. He always left his cell turned off during this time.

Phil held down the power button and was rewarded with a bright little screen full of icons. He smiled in the dark to see a fully charged battery.

He hit the power button to turn it back off.

Then he walked into Sean's office, opened the desk, and grabbed a key from the top drawer.

Rick and Esme looked to each other and then back to Phil. Esme didn't attempt to lower her voice. "Why are we still here, *pendejo*? We need to get the fuck out!"

The first Hunter crashed into the back of the house and every window shattered. The walls bulged. Bricks and limestone pushed through the sheetrock and poured into the living room.

Phil shouted, "Ten seconds!" and then bolted out of sight down a corridor.

They heard a crash and a metallic clatter and a scream of profanity from Phil, but he was good to his word. Another crash and clatter and he emerged from the corridor.

The house was collapsing around them, the ceiling falling in as joists twisted and cracked, beams giving way.

Phil yelled, "Go, go now! Out the front door!"

But they didn't need any of his encouragement; they were already halfway through the door. He followed just behind, zipping up a green nylon backpack.

They ran no more than two blocks, but their lungs and throats screamed out, and the wretched taste of blood filled their mouths and grew steadily fouler as each breath dried those traces of blood, sticking to their teeth.

They were now a block to the east of Maypole, on Bowmen Street, entering the alley behind Lloyd's house. The air was different here, somehow less harsh, less foul. And it became even less so as they neared Lloyd's back gate. It was cooler, with even a hint of moisture.

They arrived at the gate and Phil tried to quietly open it, but it was locked. He looked to his companions and saw their dead weariness. He motioned with his hands to take a drink, to pour some water on a rag and inhale it through the nose.

They didn't look any better when they'd finished, their heads still pivoted back in the direction of the sounds of Sean's house being crushed into nothing, followed by the bellowing, ear shattering roar of the Hunters.

He nodded his head, understanding. Then he motioned for Rick to cup two hands together and give him a lift up and over the fence. He went up, and painfully scraped over the top of the fence, opening new burning and itching rents in his skin. He wiped away the blood and it was dry before his hand left his skin.

Despite this, the air was decidedly better, even more so on this side of the fence. He quietly lifted the bar that locked the gate in place and let his comrades through.

The Hunters were still busy crushing Sean's house, so he hazarded a brief look around the yard with his flashlight, and his suspicions were rewarded.

While the grass and trees and bushes in the subdivision had been rendered to crumbling ruin by the dry air, somehow the riot of flowers encircling Lloyd's house were still alive. They were shriveling, and they were wasting, but they weren't dead yet.

He shone his light around and saw the big rainwater collection cisterns, remembering the fight that Lloyd had with the Homeowner's Association. Now, in this terrible moment, he understood why Lloyd had been willing to go through all of that effort over something that had seemed so very trivial and petty at the time.

Louis had theorized, and Abigail confirmed, that these flowers were somehow wards against things like the Hunters and whatever it was inside the kids that made them do that insane ululating screaming; things that were not from here, things that were from the other side.

Who the fuck is this man I've been living across the street from?

For a brief moment, it all seemed so impossible. *This can't be real. This can't be happening.* He pushed the thoughts from his head. *Stay in the present; stray from what's directly ahead of you, and you'll end up like Esme...*

He looked to them and their grave, battered faces. He nodded and turned the flashlight off. Darkness wrapped them tight and he carefully walked up the steps to the back door and tried the handle.

Open...

CHAPTER TWENTY-FOUR

LLOYD H. REYNOLDS, ESQUIRE, HAD been a daily fixture in Phil's life since he'd moved into Blackwood Estates. Every day, Phil made small talk with him as he walked Benny. He got caught up on whatever gossip Lloyd felt it necessary to impart, and liked him less for it every single day. What he hadn't known was that the entire time, the whole thing was a ruse.

It was blacker on the inside, blacker even than the unnatural darkness that pervaded the unnatural portion of Blackwood Estates that had become their unnatural prison.

He flipped his little light back on and swept it around the kitchen, his mind taking a moment to process what lay all around him, sidetracked by the odd nagging thought: *For a man so obsessed with his flower gardens, who took (what appeared to be) such immense pride in the outside of his home, every single window remained closed. I never thought about that. I never once stepped foot inside Lloyd's house, and a weirdo like him would almost certainly have invited me in.* The inside of Lloyd's house was completely hidden by heavy light-blocking drapes. This place was completely sealed off from light from outside. Not that there was any now anyway.

And at a very pedestrian level, the reason was obvious. Every single surface was painted a dead matte black. Walls, ceilings, floors. There was almost no furniture, and what furniture there was…it was completely black as well.

Rick whispered, "Why?"

Esme's voice quavered: "Serial killer."

Phil shook his head from side to side and whispered back, "I think we're looking at something there isn't a definition for. This is something completely different."

Esme shook her head back. "Bullshit. This fucker is gonna have a collection of little shoes. And we're completely unarmed."

Phil looked to Rick. "You were in the Army, right? You know how to use a gun?"

Rick nodded. "Yeah."

Phil unzipped the bag he took from Sean's, took out a shiny black pistol, and handed it to Rick. "I know the general idea, but I haven't shot a gun since summer camp when I was a kid."

For the first time, he saw Rick smile. "Fucking Austin liberals."

Phil shrugged and sighed. "Yeah, pretty much."

Rick racked the pistol, checking the chamber. "Glock 17. We're in business."

Phil looked at him hard. "If you fire that…"

Rick nodded quickly. "Yeah, I know. I understand. Last resort."

They looked around to one another, steeling themselves, and walked out into the living room. Or rather, what would have been a living room if it hadn't been completely empty, every surface painted completely black.

The dining room was more of the same.

They looked up the staircase. Black carpets, black handrails, black walls.

Rick took the lead, tactical stance, gun pointed down. They heard a dinging noise halfway up the stairs followed by a flickering of the house lights as they all came on. Blinding sodium arc lights. The kind that you would light a movie set with.

Phil shielded his eyes. "All the windows are covered. They'd have to be, right?"

Rick answered, "Somehow I don't think the Homeowner's Association would be okay with any of this, so yeah."

Even though the air was much better in this house than outside, they were beginning to notice some very strange smells.

Esme whispered, "We might be too late. Is that…"

Rick interjected, "No. It's…not a dead body. I think."

Phil shook his head, scared in an entirely new way. "Oh God no, Louis said that this is the only way out!"

Rick nodded and took the next few stairs in two bounds, and Phil followed close.

They were in a small hallway, every surface painted black. There were five doors: three to the right and two to the left.

Phil looked to Rick and Esme and exhaled hard. "Okay, cover me?"

The first door to the right was a linen closet, full of the usual stuff, but no linens.

The second was a bathroom, normal in all regards except for the fact that everything was black.

The third door to the right opened to something completely

different.

If the house lights hadn't come on, they would have seen the odd red light creeping out from under the door, and maybe stopped to consider the peculiar smell that came from this room. Not rotten, exactly, but fecal and dry.

The entire room was full of giant terrariums, each home to an enormous female black widow spider and her enormous and chaotic web, festooned with white silken orbs, each containing the piteous desiccated form of a baby mouse.

When they walked into the room, all of the spiders rushed to a tubular aperture at the top of their terrarium, eager and excited at the prospect of a terrified, squirming morsel. All of them but the few who had most recently feasted, bloated and content to dangle in their terrific webbing.

Apart from these was another gigantic terrarium, this one full of white mice, whiskers aquiver, seeming to understand some darker truth.

"Tell me he doesn't shove those up his ass," Esme gritted.

Phil didn't take his eyes away from the glass in between himself and the black widows. "I think he's breeding them to feed to the spiders."

She continued, "Taped up, claws and teeth yanked out, and shoved up his ass."

Rick shook his head, voice barely above a whisper. "Fucking sick fuck. He's been living here next to Felix and Rhonda the whole fucking time."

Esme finished his thought: "Fucking pervert faggot serial killer fuck."

Phil never stopped shaking his head, and his eyes never left the glass. "I'm pretty sure this is something completely different."

Rick nodded. "No matter what, we burn this place to the ground. Even if we're all fucked, this place burns."

Phil exhaled hard. "No objections here."

Esme cleared her throat. "You don't think he…*did something* to the girls?"

Phil kept staring at the horrible spiders. "Yeah. He did. He did something to all the kids."

Something like a growl escaped Esme's chest, and she shoved Phil against the door and hissed. He hit the door and slid down, landing on the floor. "They aren't here! They're in Port Arthur with their parents, and that's why that little monster inside your kid is even still alive!"

Rick quickly put his arms around her, gently holding her back in case she escalated her mania. "Shhh, shhh, honey. They're not here, they're safe!"

Phil was dazed. He hadn't thought about the terrible reality of Esme and the Rosales girls, of the terrible reality of Esme and little *Mary Rosales*. He'd only been thinking of their present task.

Then his mind snapped back to the present: *Where is Lloyd H. Reynolds?*

Before these thoughts could fully register, before Esme could spiral further out of control, a small plaintive voice came to them from behind the door. "A penny, a farthing, something, anything, my lord. I will be good. I will be whoever pleases you…"

Rick asked the obvious, gun up and pointing at the door: "Who the fuck is that?"

Phil and Rick's eyes met. Phil jumped to his feet and Rick lowered the gun, but kept it at the ready. Phil turned and put his hand on the knob.

Rick nodded and Phil yanked the door open. Nothing but the hallway, painted black.

Phil motioned with a quick jerk of his head and they were across the hallway, facing the first of two doors on the other side of the staircase. He exhaled, then glanced to Rick, nodding back to him. He jerked the door open. A bedroom of sorts. Nothing but piles of laundry and a hard cot.

That left one last door. From behind they heard the moaning of a little boy. "A penny, a farthing, my lord. I will be whatever you desire…"

Phil rushed forward, his back along the left wall, and glanced back to Rick, ready with the Glock in a tactical stance. He nodded, Rick nodded, and Phil grasped the knob and flung the door open.

Esme gasped, and Rick gasped. Phil swallowed hard.

There was a naked little boy, not even ten years old, on a large X-shaped crucifix. Not nailed, but held in place by manacles and a rope around his torso.

He was red with blood.

Every surface of this room was black, just like the rest of this house, but this room was covered, walls and floor, with black plastic tarpaulins. And the reason became evident very quickly.

This room was the source of the smell.

It was a rusty, meaty, rotten smell.

Blood.

The boy was covered in blood, but not his own.

There was a bucket at the base of the crucifix, and Esme walked over to it and picked it up. She stuck her nose in it and immediately dropped it, coughing and retching. The contents of the bucket, at least half-full, sloshed onto the tarp-covered floor. Blood.

110

Rick's lips moved, and a bare whisper poured out: "Oh my God, *ay dios mio...*"

Esme finished coughing, and a terrible sob came from her throat. "*Ay dios mio, ay dios mio...*"

Phil went to the boy's side, and put his hand under his chin to lift his head and clear his airway. His eyes flew open, a startling blue against his gore-soaked skin. They regarded each other as Phil's mind tried to connect the dots. The boy inhaled hard, and exhaled, "A penny, a farthing, nothing more, my lord, and I will be whoever you want for me to be. A boy, a girl, your sister, or..."

Esme screamed, shattering their silent world. "Shut up, shut up, shut up!"

Phil and Rick looked to one another in horror. Their time here was going to be much shorter than they needed it to be.

Phil whispered to the boy, "It's okay, we're going to get you out of here. What's your name, son?"

The boy's eyes were glassy and unfocused. "Terrence, Terrence Neville of..."

His eyes fluttered closed, then opened abruptly, staring at a spot opposite him. Phil's gaze followed his to the wall. Rick and Esme were already moving in that direction. There was a door behind those tarpaulins.

It was a large walk-in closet and, like everything else in this house, completely black, dominated by a large glossy maroon-red box covered in a flowing calligraphy of gold and silver hieroglyphs.

It was beautiful, it was stark, it was utterly alien.

There was a simple lever mechanism to open the lid. Esme reached down to pull the lever, but Phil spoke up. "Wait! Rick, hand me the gun. Esme... Go out there and talk to that boy."

She looked at him incredulously. "No. I want to see what this sick fuck has inside this fucking box."

Phil looked to Rick, also incredulous. Phil changed his expression ever so slightly, and Rick got it.

Rick looked over to his wife. "Honey, we don't have much time, please just..."

Esme snarled and shouldered past Phil and out of the closet. "Fucking spineless coward."

The men looked to each other; then Rick looked away. Too much pain there.

Phil cleared his throat. "Be ready."

The lever opened the box, and the two halves of the lid opened up like a flower and retracted down the sides in a silent fluid motion.

Both men inhaled hard; shock and disgust, revulsion and terrific awe.

Lloyd H. Reynolds was inside.

Unconscious. Suspended in a seat, the one next to him empty but covered in a crust of blood. The boy had been inside this box with him.

But the *horror* was something else entirely.

Lloyd was naked, but his nudity was incomplete, because his penis and testicles were missing. This nothingness was covered by a glass globe, affixed to the man by a series of leather straps, fitted flush against his skin to contain several enormous black widow spiders, fangs affixed to the stumps of his missing manhood, hideous and dangling.

Suddenly he *flickered*, like a bad signal on an old-fashioned television.

And then he vanished, with no sound.

A moment later, he reappeared. Just like that, he was back from wherever he had vanished to. Sane men, rational men, would question what they had just seen for the remainder of their days, but Phil and Rick had been through that, and knew better than to trust in the dubious havens of sanity and rationalism. They knew exactly where Lloyd H. Reynolds had vanished to.

The Space Between the Spaces.

Even though they had never been there themselves, and had no wish to go there, and had no idea where or what that Space really was, they knew it was real. They also knew that the time to ponder the imponderables was a luxury they did not possess.

They reached in, unstrapped him from his harness, and yanked Lloyd H. Reynolds out, throwing him roughly to the floor of the room, closing the door of the closet behind them.

CHAPTER TWENTY-FIVE

H E REACHED OUT WITH ONE hand, and then another, and then another and another, until he touched the horizon from one end to the other. It was curved, a sphere floating in an infinity of spheres.

Like a box full of Christmas ornaments...

They touched, the borders rolling over and over one another. All he had to do was leap out with his mind when his place inside this sphere rolled against the surface of another sphere.

All he had to do was leap and he would be free.

He could see the next one rolling his way, and the sphere he was imprisoned in rolled against it. He could see into it, a curved refraction of what it was, but enough to understand that it was a nexus, an omnidirectional world of liquid staircases flowing into an infinity of directions on an infinity of axes.

All directions.

Up, down, backward, forward, inside out.

The foyer of everywhere and everywhen.

His mind and his will were one. Never before had his focus been so acute, his purpose so clear, his desire so manifest.

But then he fell...

Down, down into a blackness of roofs and streets and lawns. He knew his own home, he knew his own yard, he knew the shingles of his own roof as they raced up toward him as he raced down, down, down to crash.

To die...

Hands.

Rough, cruel, hard, dirty hands.

And then he felt himself crash onto the floor, felt the carpet beneath and the tarpaulin, slick with blood.

His breath returned. His eyes opened.

He was spread-eagle on the floor, and Phil Nada and Rick and Esme Salazar regarded him with red eyes and bloody faces. Hair like filthy straw, faces smeared with caked-on blood and dirt.

He was naked, save for the glass globe attached by a clever series of straps to his groin. He'd had this made special. A special toy for a special purpose, to inject the narcotic venom in just the right way. A bit of genius that came to him while meditating, trying to find the first rung of the ladder that had brought him to the Sublimity.

Behind them the boy hung on his special cross. This had been another idea that had come to him while meditating. They needed to hang for a few days with no food or water, sweating and screaming out the hallucinations brought about by the black widow venom before their minds were attuned enough to join his mind and cast the box into the wilds of the Sublimity.

The blood covering the boy was to make sure that the gatekeeper knew which of them was the sacrifice and which of them was the priest.

From the looks on the assembled faces, none of these three saw his genius.

No, they saw him as something else entirely.

Esme squatted down next to him, face expressionless, and reached out to touch the globe. She tapped on the glass, and the spiders inside twitched, but didn't release their fangs from the dappled flesh of his ruined manhood.

She turned her head and looked into his eyes; then she punched him in the face. He was sure he cried out for Phil to intercede on his behalf— they were neighbors, after all—but all three fell on him with fists and feet. The blows rained down until blackness swallowed him whole.

CHAPTER TWENTY-SIX

OUT IN THE NIGHT, HE could hear the Hunters of the Outer Dark warbling their unearthly whale songs, the verses punctuated by the crump of elephantine feet. Every few moments one of them would let out a frustrated moan of such a low timbre that it rattled his teeth.

The Hunters were a block away, milling around the wreckage of poor Sean Leonard's house. Their quarry had escaped them, a thing they did not understand.

Phil waited for another of the angry moans to cover the sound of his turning the bolt on the lock of Lloyd's front door, and another moan to open it, and another yet to step outside and close the door behind him.

He said a silent prayer to a god he was quite sure had abandoned him, and slipped off his shoes to make himself even more quiet. He quickly walked up the path toward the gate in the picket fence surrounding Lloyd's house, and gingerly lifted one leg over, then the other. He glanced back at what little he could see of Lloyd's front yard. His flowers were now completely wasted, dried and brittle.

When the Hunters finished with Sean's house, this might very well be their next destination. They could have heard Esme cry out earlier. Despite the fact that they'd put Lloyd's pervert ball gag in that boy's mouth to keep him from screaming out in late-nineteenth century Cockney delirium, he was still a victim as much as they were. The Hunters would kill him where he hung. They couldn't let him go or he could and would run amok in his intoxication.

He took a deep breath of the dry, awful air and stifled a cough.

Then he risked a look over his shoulder. Lloyd's house was in between himself and the Hunters, and their titan footsteps seemed less focused on Sean's house. They'd begun to mill about.

Fucking move, dipshit.

Yes, you're all alone out here.

Yes, it's scary.

Yes, you're a beta male whose best friend is a dog.

He put one foot in front of the other and trotted ever so carefully across the asphalt of the street, feet kicking up eddies of dust. He got to the front of his house and nearly walked across the grass, but stopped himself, knowing that the dry crunching and crackling would sound like an artillery barrage. He took the walkway instead.

As he expected, the door was open, and as he expected, his house had been systematically dismantled, and none too gently. He crossed the foyer and risked a glance at the terrible form of little Mary Rosales. His feet carried him over to her, forced him to bear witness to this horror. She was dead, dried out, desiccated, covered in a pall of dust. A burning came as tears he couldn't spare filled his eyes.

There's nothing you can do about that.

And we have to get through this thing without Esme finding out or she will flip out and try to kill Benny. And Benny is keeping those evil kids away. For now.

The tears began to fall, but he didn't hear them hit the dusty floor because they evaporated before they reached it. He tried to force it from his mind, but the images came unbidden. *Esme.* As much as he hated her for the threat she posed, he couldn't escape the fact of why she posed that threat. She was human, and terrible circumstances had denied her that most basic of human desires: children.

Who would he be without Scotty? He couldn't even imagine.

He pulled himself from this fugue, through the kitchen and out the back door.

Tawana lay on the lawn chair where he'd left her, every bit as dead as Mary Rosales, every bit as dried and desiccated, and every bit as corrosive to his mind.

He squeezed his eyes shut and counted back from ten, pushing the tears and the grief away.

Phil took the little cobblestone path around the garage and squatted down next to the galvanized steel drainpipe embedded in concrete that snaked under the fence. He reached into his pocket, pulled out Sean's phone, and turned it on. Then he turned the volume all the way up and set the alarm to go off in five minutes. He removed the tube of Super Glue and affixed the phone to the inside of the pipe.

He walked back past the bodies of Tawana and Mary, across the street, over the gate, and up the walkway to Lloyd's porch.

Then he waited. The alarm would be deafening in this void of sound.

CHAPTER TWENTY-SEVEN

ESME PRODDED LLOYD ALONG WITH all the restraint that a homicidally furious lunatic could muster. Her implement was a steak knife. Each poke left a wicked puncture and a rivulet of blood that dried instantly. He was beaten and naked in his own special way, and a pair of socks filled his mouth, with a cruel band of duct tape holding them in place.

Phil remembered this, but much of their journey was simply erased by the trauma of it having been possible in the first place. By the *knowing* imparted to him.

Everything had gone according to plan. The noisy alarm on poor Sean Leonard's phone had drawn the Hunters, galloping on a herd of elephantine legs and thunderous feet. They charged right through and over Phil's already devastated house. If it was possible for there to be such a thing as a furious whale song punctuated by foghorn moans, that is what it would have sounded like.

Phil and company travelled the route they would have taken if they hadn't been detoured before. The path between the fences was now a wide-open passage strewn with the wreckage of the Hunters's pursuit of them earlier.

Then he saw it. It was beautiful really, elegant and graceful in the way it reared up, raising its trunk, up, up, up into the air, visible by the anti-luminance of the constellations inside its mass.

Legs, enormous, writhing into the air.

Mandibles to tear the firmament of heaven.

The Hunter of the Outer Dark.

His head was already turning away, so no visions came, only the idea the visions would have imparted: that he would be responsible for his son's death.

***

Their journey back through the darkness lasted mere minutes. The Hunters pounded and beat the earth, each failed attempt to dislodge Sean's noisy cell phone driving them to new heights of fury. They reared up and crashed their bulk into the earth, the vibrations rattling Jayne's windows.

Benny's eyes rolled this way and that as the house swayed. His gaze crossed Jayne's and she saw the character and intelligence behind those eyes. But never once did his head rise from Scotty's chest. His resolve was total.

Scotty and Wendy, *Louis and Abigail,* lay still, the cough syrup working its narcotic magic. Jayne didn't hear them enter the house, but Benny did. His eyes stopped roving for a moment, and he finally raised his head, tilting it to the side quizzically.

He stood silently and put himself between the children and the door. He was unalarmed, but still cautious. He knew the sounds of Phil, Rick, and Esme, and knew the sound and smell of the fourth person as well, but something was very different.

Jayne's hand went to cover her mouth as they entered the room.

Lloyd H. Reynolds, Esquire. Naked. Covered in bruises and vicious little puncture wounds. Hands bound and mouth gagged.

Dickless. Ball-less. The wreckage of his manhood covered by some kind of glass globe.

Full of black widow spiders.

The other three looked like they'd been through hell, but the astral moaning of the Hunters out in the night told her they'd been through a much worse hell than she'd learned about as a child.

The words came blurting out: "Lloyd, oh my God, what happened to you?!"

Their eyes met, and in that moment, both Jayne and Benny understood that they'd erred terribly in their estimation of Lloyd. He was far more than a man with many secrets could ever be; in fact, no longer a man at all, but a *thing* that had abandoned its basic essence to become more than any man, any human, could be.

But why? What hunger could drive a man to do this to himself?

Benny locked eyes with him, with *it,* and knew that he could never know the whys of this one's appetites. As always, he was unafraid. But being without fear for oneself is not the same as being without fear for one's charges. He breathed a warning growl for this one to know its place.

He glanced to Phil. *You shouldn't have brought this thing here. Let me kill it.*

Despite her horror and apprehension, Jayne stood, glancing down at the sleeping children, then back to Lloyd, then entered the large walk-in closet and returned with a white bathrobe. She held it up and draped it around Lloyd's shoulders, and tied it around the front, hands hesitating at the glass globe full of venomous spiders, their eyes locked the entire time, hers in understandable fear, his in fear of *consequences*.

Phil and Rick slumped against a wall and slid to the floor and Esme continued standing, glaring radioactively as Jayne led Lloyd to the bed and gently sat him down. Rick sobbed quietly, but no one spoke.

CHAPTER TWENTY-EIGHT

DID HE SLEEP? IS IT sleep to just close your eyes and hover over the horizon of dreams, but never let your feet leave the safe ground of wakefulness? Phil opened one eye to look across the big double bed at Jayne, their two children between them. Her face was a ruin of dirt and tears, blood and days old makeup. Her hair was worse.

She looked terrible.

He ran his tongue over his teeth and wondered what a person in the normal world would think about his breath. He wondered about his toothbrush back at his house, just a few blocks away. It might as well be on another continent, on another planet. When this was through and done, he told himself that he was going to walk back over here, sweep Jayne off her feet, and... He stopped that train of thought before it became any more insipid. This might not ever be through, this might not ever be done. It was more likely that they would die here.

His eyes closed hard till he saw stars. They radiated in geometric patterns, shifting from red to blue to white, and a tiny tear squeezed from between his eyelids. He felt Benny nudge him in the shins from his perch at the foot of the bed, and his head jerked up as his eyes opened, stars still streaking.

Benny knew; his big brown eyes told everything. *Phil, you have to hold it together. If not for yourself, then for Scotty. I'll do the best I can, but I'm only a dog.*

Despite himself, Phil smiled, but still wanted to cry more. He inhaled hard, though the dry air burned, and held it.

He nodded his head ever so slightly to Benny. The dog blinked slowly and looked back to Phil, then glanced over to Jayne. *No crying, Phil. Crying only leads to more crying.*

Phil turned his head to find her looking at him. He smiled and shook his head. "A beta male whose best friend is a dog?"

"No," she said softly, glancing at the lines streaked by tears through the dirt on his face.

Benny raised his head and his ears went halfway up, his eyes on Scotty, and in the next second the boy spoke, but it was Louis talking. "You have brought him here."

Jayne had been curled protectively around Wendy, but she pulled away from her daughter in a way she obviously wished was more subtle.

The boy and the girl sat up stiffly, moving their necks and shoulders this way and that. They turned to look at one another but no words passed between them.

Phil coughed, then winced as the skin tore at the corner of his mouth. "Yeah, you got to sleep through the whole thing."

Louis nodded. "The Indian woman and her man? Did they return as well?"

Jayne cleared her throat. "They're in the next room."

Louis sighed and shook his head. "Pity. She will most likely get us all killed."

Jayne yawned. "Hispanic. Not Indian. Wrong continent."

Louis paused, then motioned with his head. "He is in the closet? You have bound him securely?"

Phil nodded, disgust written across his face.

A small laugh escaped Louis. "No means of real transcendence will please those for whom the mundane is palatable. He has done something unspeakable?"

Phil and Jayne glanced to one another. Phil looked back to Louis, but Jayne answered. "*He* might not be the right word anymore."

Louis nodded. "Bring food. For us as well as…him. We need to discuss how this thing occurred, and how to undo what has been done."

CHAPTER TWENTY-NINE

THE RETARD. PHIL'S FUCKING KID. You have got to be kidding me...

But there he was, sitting upright: not running around in circles, but speaking in complete sentences. Eyes focused and looking directly into his own, something Scotty never did.

Lloyd still wore the bathrobe that Jayne had draped around him, spotted red with blood. He sat in a chair, still bound, still gagged, the glass globe still covering his crotch while the peanut gallery gaped at him like he was...

A freak! An alien! An abomination!

He wasn't sure, but he felt like he might have smiled somewhere over that last approximation. *Abomination.*

Well, it isn't just me anymore, is it? I've been joined by a halfwit.

Scotty. That was his name. Sitting there like an ugly ventriloquist's dummy, and another one right next to him. Wendy. Jayne's kid.

They regarded one another, just about five feet between them. Him tied to his chair, Scotty and Wendy upright on the bed, hands and feet bound with expensive belts and scarves. Between them, Benny sat on his hindquarters with his ears straight up, eyes punching holes right through him, trying to divine what manner of creature had been fooling him, under his very nose for the entirety of his existence.

There was curiosity, leavened by the strong desire to kill.

Phil and Jayne and Rick and Esme stood in a circle around him, Esme clutching a bloody steak knife and Rick a nine-millimeter pistol. Probably a Sig or a Glock.

Is this how the world ends, the one useful man on earth surrounded by a mob of halfwits without the ability to see beyond their need to eat, shit, and fuck?

"Yes, that was my experience as well. I, too, was caught in *flagrante delicto*, and carted off. I went to Bedlam. You, I fear, won't make it that far."

The retard just spoke to me.

No grunting, chirping, screaming, or absurd gesticulation. Complete sentences with ordered thought.

Lloyd looked to Phil. "How…"

Then he looked back to Scotty, eyes wide in newfound appreciation and appraisal. He'd seen mountains on impossible worlds and upside down gods inside inverted realities, but this was something different.

Phil didn't answer. Something like pain was painted on his face. Pain, and fear, and revulsion. Not revulsion at the eunuch tied to the chair, but revulsion at the puppeteer's voice behind his son's words.

Lloyd looked back to Scotty, his mouth about to ask the question again, but he stopped himself. Stupid questions were for people like those surrounding them. No, he'd understood that there were others like himself; he'd just never spoken to one of them.

The one inside Scotty spoke first in a haughty English accent. *"Lorsque les étoiles s'alignent, nous ouvrirons une porte sur l'espace entre les espaces."*

Lloyd controlled his facial muscles so that dismay wouldn't make him look weak. He didn't know Greek or French or any other language besides English. He'd never thought that he'd meet another like himself, and while it wasn't surprising that they'd speak French, he felt out of his depths.

Esme and Rick looked to one another. Rick shook his head and squinted. "Something about space and doors?"

Lloyd responded, "I don't speak French, but you do speak English. It seems like we have a few things to discuss. What is your name?"

He watched Scotty and Wendy turn and regard one another, Scotty shaking his head in some kind of communication with her.

He turned back and faced Lloyd with a question of his own. "How do you not speak French? You must, or you would not…"

"I didn't use a book. I don't have one."

"Then how do you travel the Space Between the Spaces?"

"I built a…device."

Louis looked stunned and turned to Phil as if to ask a pointed question, then stopped and turned back to Lloyd. "Was this a contrivance of science?"

Lloyd smiled inwardly. Lying came naturally to him. "Yes."

Phil shook his head. "He's lying. He's no more of a scientist than I am. He's a lawyer."

Scotty's head swiveled back to Lloyd and fixed him with a steely stare.

Phil continued, "Lloyd, we've got you tied to a chair. So you can play nice with Louis, or I might let Benny lead the conversation."

At this Benny put his muzzle within inches of Lloyd's face, providing a close-up of his teeth.

But Lloyd smiled, and Louis shook his head and sighed. He should have thought about that. He should have warned them not to give this one his name. Names are important. Names are powerful.

Lloyd ignored Benny's deadly threat. "So, Louis, the answer is no and no. I don't speak French, and I don't have a book. I take it you learned from a book?"

Louis sneered. "Books. Plural."

Lloyd asked, "And do these books have names as well?"

Esme had had enough. She poked Lloyd right in the temple with the steak knife. Blood gushed, and Lloyd was about to scream, but Esme had him by the hair, her knife poking the delicate skin of his eyelid. "You speak when you're spoken to, thing."

Phil wanted to jump, to do something, but knew how that turned out in the past. They couldn't afford this, not now.

Jayne spoke first. "Esme, honey, it's not worth it. We need him. At least, we might. Maybe later we can…"

Esme interrupted: "Shut it, *fresa*." She turned her eyes back to Lloyd. "Did you touch my nieces? Did you touch the Morales girls? Felix and Rhonda? Did you? Did you, you piece of fucking filth?"

Blood was now pouring from Lloyd's eyelid, down his face, and dripping…

There was a loud bang as a rock slammed into the front door.

Elizabeth Cromwell was back.

CHAPTER THIRTY

"WHERE IS LOUIS VILLEFORT? BRING him out now."
Elizabeth Cromwell, and every other one of these horrible
children, was even more piteous than they were just a day
before. Their eyes shot red, skin scabbed and dirt-caked, hands stained
black with blood. Their clothes clung to them with grime or hung in
tatters, hair matted and falling out in clumps. But none of this decrepitude
had stilled their ferality. It magnified it.

In a word, they were possessed.

Phil, Rick, and Benny faced the crowd again across a distance of
meters in Jayne's front yard. This time, Rick held the pistol at his side for
all to see. But even the fact of an armed man and an attack dog didn't
seem to sway them.

Rick coughed and shook his head. Phil tried a confident laugh. "You
need to set an appointment, *Penny*."

"You reek of inferiority, little man. You only survive due to the
charity of others and the coddling falsity of this world."

Rick shook his head again. "Damn, kid, you need therapy."

But Elizabeth Cromwell wasn't done with Phil. "Even now you
cringe and shrink from the words of a little girl. An imbecile that begets
imbeciles. Do not attempt to bandy words with me. Bring Villefort."

Phil's façade wasn't what he hoped it would be, and he found Rick
looking at him, then elbowing him to snap him out of his fugue. He
cleared his throat. He coughed and spit. "You got ten seconds. Say
something to keep us from walking back inside."

Elizabeth smiled, creasing lines into her filthy face. "Perhaps Tio
Ricardo would like to go get Tia Esme?"

A whole different kind of expression took over Rick. His war face.
The gun was up and pointed right at Elizabeth's forehead. "The fuck did
you say?"

"It seems, Phil, that I've got Tio Ricardo's attention. Be a dear and go get Tia Esme."

Phil could hear Rick's knuckles tightening around the grip of his pistol. "What the fuck are you saying, goddamnit?"

Phil only managed to stammer, "Rick, Rick, gimme the gun, go...go inside..."

Elizabeth smiled kindly and called in a happy little voice, "Andrea? Tristina? Come, and bring sweet Monica and Juanita with you! They'd love to talk to Tio Ricardo."

The crowd parted and Monica and Juanita Rosales walked to the front, holding hands and smiling as if for Sunday school cake and ice cream.

The front door banged open and Esme launched through, growling and cursing.

Just as when Elizabeth had baited Jayne, Esme charged headlong out into the yard, and Rick tackled her. He was then battered and beaten and cursed as a worthless coward by his wife for the crime of saving her, even though this time there was no phalanx of lawn tools and broken pool cues to impale her.

Elizabeth laughed and laughed.

Eventually Rick was able to cajole Esme back to the porch, but not before his arms were rent with scratches and skin was split on his face. Esme lay weeping on the concrete, the tears drying before they even formed.

Soon Elizabeth stopped laughing. "You must be Tia Esme. I have been told of your abiding love for your nieces. All *three* of them." She let that hang in the foul air for a moment. "Pity sweet little Mary won't be joining us today."

Esme sobbed. "I'll give you anything, I'll do anything..."

Elizabeth nodded. "I sympathize. I do. But there is precious little you could give me that would be worth—"

Phil found his voice. "Shoot her, Rick. Shoot her! It's not a little girl, it's a monster, and she'll kill us all!"

Elizabeth laughed again. "The gelding might have ulterior motives, don't you think?"

Phil screamed now. "Rick, shoot her!"

But the fight had drained from Rick. He went pale as a cold realization crept over him. His niece was dead, and he was about to add another little girl to the death toll. He aimed down the barrel of the pistol, squinting, sweating, crying, lips forming the words, "I can't do it, I can't do it, I can't do it."

Phil reached over and put his hand over Rick's gun, gently taking it from him but keeping it pointed at Elizabeth. Rick simply stood shaking, tears pouring down his face, leaving swollen red trails across his cheeks.

But Esme had stilled, and stared out at her nieces. "Where is Mary? Monica, Juanita, answer me," she said quietly, and then a little louder. "Where is Mary?" And then again, and again, louder and louder, until her words blurred into a single imprecation. "WHERE IS MARY?"

And then she stopped speaking as Elizabeth held her gaze. "Oh, Tia, Tia, Tia. You poor thing. But I don't wish to be the bearer of bad news. You should ask Phil, being that he is the owner of this dog."

Esme turned to Phil, Rick turned to Phil, and Benny rotated his body to face the crowd, without his back turned to Rick and Esme.

His big brown eyes turned to Phil. *I'm so sorry, Phil, I'm so sorry. Be ready. Scotty needs you.*

The world pressed in on Phil, his breathing became shallow, and he suddenly felt cold, not hot. The voices of Esme and Rick blurred and stretched and hung in the dead air with the dirt and the dust. Their mouths moved, but all he could hear was his own pulse hammering in his chest.

Rick was holding Esme back as she thrashed and reached for Phil, her head turning and screaming something to Elizabeth, to her nieces standing with frozen rictus grins, ropes of black ichor hanging from their chins, forming minute blasphemies before they hit the ground and scuttled away.

Phil saw himself from the outside. Hapless, foolish, absurd. Not equal to the task, not worthy of the respect of his wife, just a man who had blundered too far to swim back to the safety of the shore.

The pistol hung pointed at the ground.

Benny barked and growled, turning back and forth between the crowd of kids and Rick struggling to hold Esme back.

But Elizabeth's words cut through the pounding in Phil's ears.

"It was the wolf, Tia. He tore Mary's throat out and Phil left her to die."

Rick's muscles went slack, and for a brief moment Phil saw the full measure of Rick's loss. He'd lost his wife. She was gone, and she wasn't coming back. And in that second he saw the measure of Esme's loss as well. She'd lost the children and the only life she'd ever known or wanted.

The knife in her hand slammed once into Rick's belly, and his arms instinctively fell to cover the wound as he collapsed to his knees. In the next motion, she pulled the knife free and lurched toward Phil. "Liar! Murderer!"

Benny launched at her, a fury of steel-grey fur, taking her to the ground while the knife took him in the ribcage. It was over for Esme in seconds.

Phil fell over backward, his finger jerking the trigger over and over as a tide of feral children swept toward Rick and Esme.

Phil slammed his back against the front door and his other hand found the doorknob, turning and then stumbling backward inside as the dying screams of Rick and Benny eclipsed his mind.

He slid to the floor, dropping the pistol, locking the door with his free hand.

Two thoughts crossed into his shock.

I just shot a little girl named Penny, and God knows how many of those other little kids. I am a beta male whose best friend was a dog.

CHAPTER THIRTY-ONE

"YOU, SIR, ARE A LIAR. There is no means of craft that you could employ to create such a device without knowledge gained from a book. This device you have devised is a contrivance of science. Perhaps by the year 1944, man has transcended his vulgarity…"

For the first time in a very long time, Louis wanted to rethink his words. Yes, this man was a liar, but something of his unfathomable deviancy spoke of understandings beyond what the sciences could supply man. Maybe there was some truth…

"1944?" It was the blonde-haired woman. The one Phil clearly wished to fuck. The mother of Wendy, the host of Abigail.

Louis was annoyed. Why would a dolt like this even be allowed to speak in a future where man could transcend the spheres?

He ignored her and pressed on, berating this man, this former man, tied to a chair.

He, it, Lloyd, whatever it was, spoke as well. "1944?"

"Yes, liar, 1944. The year in which we would currently reside if we were not stranded in this planar anomaly!"

Lloyd's brow's creased. "They're lying, you know. I don't know why, but they're lying to you. It's not 1944. That was more than sixty years ago."

Jayne looked confused, completely out of her depth. "Shut the fuck up, Lloyd."

Lloyd cocked his head and turned to Jayne. "You are…stupid, at best, Jayne. Probably nice to look at, but apparently not enough to keep your husband."

She looked down and muttered, "You don't know what you're talking about, Lloyd. You're just a mean…"

She trailed off.

Lloyd turned back to Louis. "Not very bright, that one. Must be infuriating having such a dolt as your prison guard."

Louis scoffed. "Do not try to ingratiate yourself with me, *thing*."

Lloyd's face brightened. "Finally! Someone who truly gets it. Unlike poor Jayne's wayward husband. He's more one that takes it." He turned to Jayne. "Did you know that he got drunk and showed up at my door one time wanting to suck my dick? He begged me to fuck his ass. I turned him away because, well, you know… I'm all out of dicks."

Jayne's face fell further, and she stood up and walked to the bathroom.

Lloyd's expression became full. *Perfect.*

He looked Louis in the eye. "I am a thing. I've never wanted what others want. Never even cared for what they think. I always knew there was more to life, so I searched and I found it."

He let that thought hang in the air.

Louis shrugged. "What of it?"

Lloyd continued, "In all the world, in all the worlds, here you are, and here I am. I'm guessing you've never met another one like us either?"

Louis said nothing.

Lloyd looked him up and down. "The box requires two minds to operate it. I've never been joined by another like myself. I wonder what depths of the Sublimity we could find?"

Louis glanced down at his bonds, then glanced to Lloyd as Jayne walked back into the room. It was obvious she'd been crying, and she didn't make eye contact with Lloyd or Louis.

Lloyd glanced down again at his bonds and nodded ever so slightly to Louis. "You know exactly what I am. And here we are. I have no reason to lie to you."

It was agreed.

And a little face appeared at the window.

And then another, and another…

The window shattered and little faces poured through.

Jayne screamed, and wrapped her arms around her bound daughter to carry her away, even as her daughter's teeth sank into her neck again and again.

It was the strangest sensation, how her legs lost feeling and she felt the floor rising up to meet her. Her eyes fixed on her daughter as the other children cut Wendy free, and they all smiled their sweet little children's smiles. Guileless, pure. Just as she remembered them to be. They knelt around her, and she felt an odd sensation: her daughter's face wasn't her daughter's face anymore. And the other little boy, Scotty, that wasn't his face. And the words that came out of his mouth weren't his either…

"Kill her. Leave this one."

And Wendy smiled.

CHAPTER THIRTY-TWO

PHIL'S EARS HISSED WITH A kind of static he hadn't heard since he'd figured out that he needed to start wearing earplugs when he went to see live music. A little smile crossed his face at the memory. He'd been in his late twenties, Casey and he still lived in a little apartment off of Riverside. They'd ridden their bikes to the show, and afterward almost wrecked on the way home. He'd asked her when they got home if he was really that drunk but didn't hear her reply.

He saw her lips moving but…nothing.

He realized that he couldn't hear. Well, he could hear, but it was mostly static.

He remembered liking that he could still understand her because of her smiles. All night they laughed about it, and when he woke up the next day his hearing was back. But mostly he remembered her smile, locked in his mind, a snapshot of who she was and who they were.

He felt the door push against his back and his hand went up to check the lock. Yep, it was locked.

His hands went to the little button next to the grip on the pistol and the magazine popped out. Clean and efficient.

How many bullets had it held? How many times had he pulled the trigger? Did he have another magazine upstairs in that backpack he took from Sean's house?

He started to get up on his feet and his legs nearly gave out. The air was terrible, each breath its own kind of injury, each exhale its own kind of insult. He'd never been this tired before. Not that he could remember. He'd never felt so weak and tired, like he could sleep and sleep, and if he never woke, well, that would be just fine.

He realized he'd been sitting there with his eyes closed when they snapped open and focused up the stairs to where Scotty and Jayne and Wendy waited.

Louis and Elizabeth and Abigail.

He stood up to his full height and did a quick glance out the window.

He wished he hadn't. It looked like Rick's final act was to throw himself atop his wife, and all the while the children had worked on him.

He'd loved, and he'd lost.

"I'm so sorry, Rick. I'm so sorry this happened to you. I'm so sorry about everything that happened to you."

There were seven kids laying on the ground, big red spots on their clothes and faces. Phil's hand went to cover his mouth and his eyes opened so wide it hurt. He'd killed them.

There were still about ten kids gathered around something in the yard.

One of them looked up, and then they all looked up and simultaneously they all let out one of those screeches, those unreal bird calls, and began heading in his direction.

His other hand came to the fore, holding the pistol, and they stopped. And then they all ran. They'd learned all they needed to know about modern guns.

He walked out to the lawn to collect Benny. Esme's knife still jutted from his ribcage. When he reached down to touch the sticky red fur, he felt Benny move ever so slightly, and a small keening whine came from his throat.

What they'd done to him was unspeakable. They'd tied ropes to his paws to pull him spread-eagled; then they opened him up to slowly turn him inside out.

Phil saw a spark behind Benny's eyes. *I tried, Phil. I fought them.*

He put the pistol under his friend's chin. "You did good, boy, you did good."

The pistol banged once and the static in his ears got louder.

He turned and looked up at the window and saw Louis looking down on him from behind Scotty's eyes. There was nothing there but contempt. He blinked back the tears that would only make his eyes burn more, only release more scalding rivulets that would cross the dirty terrain of his face before evaporating.

A beta male whose best friend was a dog. A beta male whose wife dropped him like a bad habit the second it became an option. A beta male who wasn't equal to the task.

His mind crept back to the here and now and did the math. If Louis was standing at that window looking down at him, that meant he'd gotten loose. And if he'd gotten loose…

No haste would change what happened up in that room in his absence, so he didn't run. He also had enough sense left to know that gun or no gun, haste could lead to his death if the kids had set up an ambush. So he walked slowly, and opened the door slowly, and to the best of his ability mimicked the good guys in the books that made him so much money.

He held the pistol in some semblance of a tactical stance. He walked up the stairs, checking the corners and behind himself. He made it to Jayne's bedroom. The door was locked. He kicked it open. Doors in suburban houses are bullshit.

What he'd seen out on the lawn had numbed him to horror, but he was still taken aback by the sight of little children lapping up blood as it poured from a corpse hanging upside down.

He didn't want to shoot any more children, but the finger on the trigger made the decision for him when the first child looked up and let out one of those inhuman bird screeches.

Wendy.

The other four children bolted for the open window and were gone, their little shoes beating a tattoo as they sprinted over the rooftop and away, all ululating in that mindless way. All except for Louis, who stood at the window still looking down at the horrid battlefield that was Jayne's front yard.

Lloyd was still tied to the chair, alive.

Louis turned to regard him. "You're a survivor, Phil. Pity the same can't be said for others."

The static still burned in Phil's ears from the deafening sound of gunfire, but he heard enough to know what Louis was saying. He'd watched Scotty's mouth try for years to form words, so he'd gotten pretty good at it.

Phil didn't say anything. There really was nothing to say.

Louis looked him fully in the eye, something his son could never have done. "But the question, the real question, is whether you'd be willing to die that your son might live."

Phil looked at the floor, lost. "You're going to get in that box with Lloyd and teleport out of here."

Louis looked at him quizzically, appraising.

Phil looked up to Lloyd. "You'll raise my 'retard son' as your own?"

Lloyd tried to look contrite. "I give you my word, Phil."

Phil swallowed and nodded slowly. "He's *autistic*."

A scared look appeared on Lloyd's face, but didn't last long. There was a flash and roar, and his brains splattered all over the fine mahogany armoire behind him.

Louis and Phil looked at one another across the room for several minutes, until some modicum of hearing returned.

"Phil, I want you to know that even though I was unaware that this man's mode of traversing the spheres was possible, that the Space Between the Spaces could be known in this fashion, I can probably negotiate this device, this 'box,' as he called it."

"You ever hear the old Indian story about the frog and the scorpion?"

"This is no time for aphorism or…"

Louis was interrupted by a deep rumbling from beneath the earth as the house bucked beneath their feet. He looked out in panic as his control vanished and Scotty reappeared, terrified.

"Dadday! Dadday! Dadday!" he screamed over and over; then he fell and crawled across the swaying floor to his father. Phil held him close and fiercely, and their tears mingled as his son rubbed his face against his, as if trying to reassure himself in this way that he really was here, that he really was here in his father's arms.

Phil sobbed over and over. "I'll never let you go, I'll never leave you."

But as the earth ceased its calamities, Scotty's body stiffened and Louis returned.

Phil pushed him to a safe distance away, then turned him around, pinning him to the floor. He carefully unbuckled his belt and tied Louis' legs together. "You're not going anywhere with my son."

Louis didn't try to run; he merely rolled over and sat upright. He held his hands up, letting Phil know he wasn't going to try. "No. I'm not. But you will be coming with us."

Phil coughed from the emotion and exertion. "You're damn straight I am."

He slumped back as the exhaustion of unrelenting horror sapped his strength. He shook his head as another minor rumble shook the floor. "What was that? And why did you lose control? We're nowhere near the edge."

Louis' face slackened, the muscles losing control for a moment during the tremor, and he gasped. "When you killed that one, the binding that holds the pages of our story began to unravel. This place is tied up in him. And now that he is gone, this place will follow. We are out of time."

Phil squeezed his eyes shut and breathed hard in the vile air. "You can…fly that thing? That box he made?"

Louis was on his feet. "Yes. We should not tarry. We must get there."

Phil shook his head. "You don't know where it is, and it takes two to work. There are two seats in it. One adult, one child. It won't work with another of these kids. You need me, and I need Scotty."

Louis paused, sat down on the floor, and looked Phil in the eye. Even after all that had happened, his son's eyes, even if they weren't truly his own, tore at his soul. Scotty was autistic, and couldn't look into his eyes. "Phil, I swear to you by all the gods of the abyss, that they might take me. I swear to you this: Scotty will become whole. The Sublimity, the Servitor that we are bound to, will take his frailty and he will become more than he could ever be!"

The house shook again, longer and harder, and again Louis lost his grip and Scotty emerged from behind Louis' icy mask. "Hep, Dadday! Hep, Dadday, hep!"

Phil leapt to his feet and released the belt strap that held Jayne upside down, and her body crashed to the floor where Scotty couldn't see it. He reached down and grabbed the belt, and another one, and wobbled over to Scotty as the world swayed. He gently looped it around Scotty's knees and around his chest to hold his arms down.

He tried for a happy, reassuring smile, but was certain he looked insane. He did it anyway. "Hi, buddy! Whoa, this is funny!" He giggled and picked up Scotty and kissed his cheek. "Let's go take a walk! Whaddaya say, Scotty?"

Scotty looked scared and uncertain. Phil turned the silly up to ten. "Oh boy, I can't wait! This is gonna be fun! Whoa!" He did an exaggerated stagger in the wobbling room. "I'm gonna have to carry you, but I love carrying you, buddy!"

"Bennay? Bennay?"

Phil almost choked. "He's at home, buddy. Let's go home."

CHAPTER THIRTY-THREE

THERE WAS A RUMBLING, CRUMBLING sound nearby, and certainly too close for Phil's comfort, but human comfort was out of the question anymore. He held Scotty, alternating between limp and convulsing, and looked out the rear window of Jayne's kitchen. He'd smeared what remained of the Vaseline on his face and Scotty's, over the exposed places on his arms and his son's. He had the green nylon backpack from poor Sean's house on his back, bottles of water inside.

This rumbling and crumbling sound wasn't another of the earthquakes, but something else. He could see a plume of dust in the distance, kicking even more dirt into the already intolerably dusty air. In the intervening minutes, not even an hour since he'd blown Lloyd's brains out, everything about this place was coming apart. Their little world, this island in the Space Between the Spaces that held Blackwood Estates, was dying. There hadn't been another one of the earthquakes, but rather a continuous tremor and shake, punctuated by the rumbling.

It wasn't even close to nightfall, but already the light was draining from this place. It didn't go pitch black, but simply faded to a half-light.

Right now, he looked into Scotty's face, but it was Louis staring back. They looked out at the plume, but neither spoke; they were both certain they knew what this plume meant.

From out of the ground, one of the Hunters of the Outer Dark heaved its caterpillar mass upward into the sky, mandibles separating to emit one of the titanic trumpeting whale-song roars of dominance over this dying island. Phil placed a protective hand over his son's face, even if it wasn't his son behind that face. Then he averted his eyes.

Louis didn't struggle or object. From several other points of the compass they could hear, they could feel, that other Hunters were burrowing out of the earth. The one they'd just watched emerge curled over and dove into the earth, burrowing back downward. They were destroying this place.

"We need to move now. I don't think it's going to be an issue of remaining silent."

Louis exhaled hard. "Agreed. But as before…"

Phil nodded. "It's not going to be comfortable."

He held up Lloyd's pervert ball gag, and Louis nodded. Phil began putting it on, but stopped, shaking his head. Then he threw it away. "I can't. I don't want anything that deviant touched to…" He shook his head again. "Let's just go."

And he opened the door into the pandemonium of Blackwood Estates. He twisted the cap off one of the water bottles and poured it on Scotty's face, then let him drink the rest. He saved the last swallow for himself, then steeled himself and ran to the gate at the back of the yard, opened it and ran down between the corridor of fences to the place where it had been crushed away on their last trip out here.

He took out another bottle and they drank it in seconds, then poured the rest in their eyes to wash out the dirt. He looked to his left, at Sean's flattened home, and squeezed his eyes shut and said a brief prayer of thanks for his old friend. He didn't deserve the fate that had befallen him. No one here did, except Lloyd. He deserved it.

The wreckage of Sean's home began to rise upward and fall away as another of the Hunters clawed out of the ground, a silhouette of a titan caterpillar, full of anti-stars from an anti-cosmos. It turned its cyclopean head in their direction as hundreds of elephantine legs tasted the air of this place.

Scotty convulsed and retched. Phil ducked down behind a fence and put a hand over the boy's mouth, but realized that Louis was still in control and Scotty wasn't going to scream, but instead began vomiting. A ceaseless fountain of tiny, piteous infant rabbits, far more than could have conceivably fit within his stomach. They writhed, their smell penetrating even the dryness of this air.

Phil didn't wait, because he knew exactly what gazed at his back, with only a flimsy wooden fence in between. He stood quietly, his sounds masked by the constant rumbling, and dashed to another expanse of standing fence just in time to see the caterpillar shape of the Hunter pull down the fence, and a proboscis emerge from its face to lap up the infant rabbits. He averted his gaze and kept running.

**

By the time they reached the open back fence of Lloyd's house, Phil's nose was pouring blood. He collapsed from sheer physical pain and exhaustion. Scotty hung limp in his arms and weakly opened his eyes. "Mommy? Mommy come home?"

It was Scotty, at least for a blessed moment.

Phil closed his eyes, then opened them to look at his son's face. "Yes, Mommy's coming home. We're going to go meet her there!"

But it wasn't Scotty now. "You shouldn't lie to him, Phil. When the Servitor has made him whole, he will remember."

Phil opened another bottle and poured it over his face to clean his eyes of the dirt. He breathed in and out, hard, in the terrible air. Then he poured some over Scotty's face and wiped away the dirt and the blood from his nose. "He's gonna remember? Will he remember how his mother…"

Louis finished his sentence. "How his mother abandoned him because she didn't wish to be inconvenienced by a dullard any further?"

Phil shook his head to ward off the rage. "That's not true, she just…"

Louis scoffed. "I escaped from Bedlam, Phil. All of the morons thought that one fine day Mommy and Daddy would come and retrieve them. At least the insane had no such illusions."

Phil couldn't speak. He could only shake his head in tiny denials of what he was hearing.

Louis smiled and let out a little laugh. "You will thank me for sparing you this little embarrassment."

Even though he knew better, Phil blurted out, "How could you? How could you say…"

But he didn't finish. Louis dismissed this with a roll of his eyes. "Phil, please. You know where it ends. He and I will become one in the fullness of time, and he will be whole. Complete. Not the broken thing with a broken mind that you keep."

"Broken thing?"

"Yes, Phil."

"Broken thing…"

"I was old, Phil, and my experiments fruitless. I was lost. Another crossed the firmament to knock me from my perch, and I fell to this place, only to find what I sought."

Phil's lips moved now, but he barely whispered: "Broken thing…"

Louis nodded. "I, too, was a broken thing, old and frail, awaiting my death in Bedlam, my experiments failed. But I had not sharpened my blade down Whitechapel way for all those years in vain. Spilled blood had accumulated its weight, and the balance tipped in my favor. We opened the gate and stepped through. And now I save your son when you clearly could not."

"Who the fuck are you? *What* the fuck are you?"

Louis smiled and winked. "You may think me a curse, but I am Providence."

There was a cavernous booming noise, the sound of a world collapsing in upon itself. Scotty's body went limp and jerked weakly. His strength was gone. Phil held him close and could feel Scotty's heart hammering like some mad timpani, an arrhythmia speaking the refrain to the earthquake's rumble.

Scotty made a gagging and retching sound, and more pathetic abominations poured from his mouth. This time it was a reeking spray of blind and barely formed kittens that crashed onto the pavement behind Lloyd's house, terrible innocents born to die seconds after birth.

Phil knew this world was going to be no more, and very shortly.

He also knew the smell would draw a Hunter to feast.

He stood, clutching Scotty, and trotted the short distance to the mouth of the alley to look around the bulk of Lloyd's house at the border of the sky beyond. It was grey and indistinct as before, its uniform greyness making it impossible to judge its height, but one glance over the wreckage of his house across the street showed that the edge of the clouds—the "Erasure," as Louis had called it—was much, much closer.

It looked like the border was now in his back yard.

The world was constricting around them, and as the Hunters bored through the earth like worms through an apple, this place weakened and collapsed further in upon itself.

Phil stared at the crushed ruin of his home, everything covered in dust, until he saw the bright green plastic of Scotty's Pharmphonic peeking through the layer of grime. His feet carried him forward in his delirium.

Louis frantically but weakly pushed back at him, his arms and legs shaking, his control fading as each footstep took them closer to Phil's house.

"Phil... Good God, man... Go back, this place will be lost... We must away..."

But Phil's feet had carried him to stand in the grass of his front yard, dead and covered with a thick layer of dust. He bent down to pick up the Pharmphonic, and walked around the house, and up the driveway, all the while with Louis kicking and thrashing, ever weakening as he stepped into the back yard. He glanced at the place where Tawana would have been, but her final resting place was buried beneath the wreckage of his home.

"I'm sorry, Tawana. I should have been a better man."

Louis gasped, losing control of Scotty's mouth. "Your son, do not fail your son, I can..."

Phil felt the tear burn down his cheek. "You can't fix what isn't broken, Louis."

He walked over to the swing and set Scotty down. He'd stopped convulsing, and moved slowly in the languid way that he often did when awakening from a dream. Mere feet behind them, the cloud face, the Erasure, stretched from the ground up to the sky.

Phil listened closely. Despite the tumuli of this collapsing world, he heard the sound of the great ocean, the gently lapping waves that lay beyond the Erasure.

He turned and walked the few feet back to the swing and picked up Scotty and held him close.

Scotty opened his eyes. "Dadday?"

Phil allowed the tears to come, and Scotty lifted a finger and traced over the skin of his face. "Dadday love. Dadday love."

Phil nodded and let out a little laugh. "Yes, Daddy loves you."

Scotty smiled and picked up the Pharmphonic from the bench of the swing. He pulled the string. *"Dogs say woof woof..."*

Scotty smiled again and then looked to Phil, perplexed. "Bennay?"

Phil nodded again.

Scotty looked at him. "Mommy? Mommy come home?"

Phil nodded. "We're gonna go meet Mommy. Mommy and Benny."

Phil stood and took Scotty's hand, and they walked to the cloud face.

Acknowledgments

I WOULD LIKE TO ACKNOWLEDGE, first and foremost, the patience and good cheer of Scarlett R. Algee. It must also be noted that Sean Leonard made *Blackwood Estates* a better story, so I had to kill him. I'd also like to acknowledge the support of Brett Talley, Curtis Lawson, Mike Duke, Tristan Thorne, Michelle Garza, Rich Hawkins, Chris Payne, Don Noble, Graeme Reynolds, Philip Fracassi and most of all, my wife.

About William Holloway

WILLIAM HOLLOWAY IS A HORROR novelist from the great state of Texas. He is published by Horrific Tales UK and JournalStone. His titles with Horrific Tales include *Lucky's Girl* (2014), *The Immortal Body* (2015), and *Song of the Death God* (2017). His JournalStone titles are *The Abyssal Plain: The R'lyeh Cycle* (with Brett J. Talley, Michelle Garza, Melissa Lason, and Rich Hawkins, 2019) and *Blackwood Estates* (2020).

www.ingramcontent.com/pod-product-compliance
Lightning Source LLC
Chambersburg PA
CBHW031454260626
47154CB00017B/2814